# DON'T AS[K]

## Buy Another Copy Of

## Don't Ask, Don't Tell

## For Your Girlfriend

Find Don't Ask, Don't Tell At...

Amazon.com, in all formats or can be ordered

directly from

SoundsWrite Entertainment

www.dahnimac.com

Contact Dahni or book Dahni to DJ at your party at

http://facebook.com/dahni.mcphail

dahnimcphail@yahoo.com

www.dahnimac.com

# Don't Ask, Don't Tell

Copyright © 2007 by Dahni McPhail

Dahni McPhail Books, Inc.

All rights reserved. No part of this book may be reproduced or transmitted in any form or by any means, electronic or mechanical, including photocopying, without permission in writing from the publisher.

ISBN: 978-0-6152-0878-7

Printed in the United States of America on acid-free paper.

First Edition

Editor in Chief: K.T. Ewing

Editing Team: Anwei D. Kilgore, Wesley Kilgore, Felicia Griffin, Ebony Queen Adkins, Deborah Moore, Faye Anderson

Cover Designer: Book of Bookwormdesigns.com

**Dahni McPhail**

For Lillie, Thelma, Mae, Diahann, Kay

My Leading Ladies

And

For the woman

Who said,

"Baby, tell me a story"

### Dahni McPhail

Have you ever been killed? It makes you focus. Many things come into perspective when you feel your life seeping from a hole in your chest. This revelation came after I ended up caught in the crossfire while doing my part to keep chivalry alive. The searing pain immediately changed my thoughts about gallantry. However, it was too late to un-do the damage. My girlfriend was the last thing on my mind before I departed. I watched as she stifled her hysteria and spoke clearly to make sure the German dispatcher understood her the first time. She was trying to get them to come save me. "Shots fired. Two fatalities, one severely wounded. Send help, now!"

"Two fatalities?" I thought. "Yep, I'm really dead."

Taking you back is the only way I can sensibly bring you up to this fateful day. Therefore, here we go. The events leading to my death started when I was eighteen. My sister left for basic training, and her Recruiting Sergeant saw me as her next entrant.

Sergeant Fitzgerald. She was a pint-sized ball of fire who lived, breathed, and probably dreamed only of the United States Military. She thought being in the military was a greater idea than sliced bread, and told amazing soldier stories that made me want to see what she was talking about firsthand. She is the reason why I am lying here on the floor apologizing to Jesus for my wrongs and trying to barter my way into heaven. Sergeant Fitzgerald didn't kill me. She just brought me to the altar. The clock started ticking toward my untimely demise as soon as I raised my right hand in that Military Entrance Processing Station.

I remember the night I left. I choked back tears as I said, "See you," to my parents. They got up early to watch me get in my recruiter's car to go serve my country.

As Sergeant Fitzgerald pulled off she said, "That's the first time I've seen that around here." I could barely speak.

"Seen what?"

"Well, in this area most kids do this on their own. They come into the military without any parents to support them."

*In this area*. . . She meant "in the ghetto." I hail from one of the ten poorest cities in the United States and there are not a lot of fathers living in households. Most mothers work all the time or are at the bar. Seeing both my parents standing on the porch waving goodbye to me at three in the morning was different. "My parents always make sure I'm OK," was all I could manage to say.

Sergeant Fitzgerald reached down, brought my hand to her mouth and kissed it. "I'll make sure you're OK too."

Sergeant Fitzgerald knew something I didn't know at the time. I didn't question the kiss then, but now I know why she did it. My persona made her comfortable enough to do something like that to me. Naiveté made me ignore the obvious and think she was trying to console me as I was leaving home for the first time. Reality is she peeped my hold card."

I put aside the electric shock that zinged all the way up my arm and down into my pants too. I didn't know I was supposed to pursue the feeling then. Thinking back, I realize she ignited a flame that burned until I died. Ole Sergeant Fitzgerald, the cradle robber. She was my first lesbian encounter.

*

The bus pulled up at the training reception station and one dazed and confused little girl (and a busload of others) entered a brand new world. I was scared shitless. They ushered us into the lobby of a big concrete building and put us in the soldier assembly line. By the end of the first day, I resembled a soldier. I learned acronyms, phrases and heard orders like never before.

## Don't Ask, Don't Tell

I was hooked on the environment, the structure and all the different people. It amazed me how hundreds moved through the hallways from station to station in such an orderly and timely fashion. The drill sergeants were clean cut and professional. The people who worked in the offices were organized and efficient. Quite different from my parents' house, but still, I felt like I was home! I decided to become a drill sergeant at that moment. That would happen later. Right now I was about to be drilled. Literally. . .

After two more days of reception and integration, we shipped to training in a cattle truck: a big white, truck that transports cows or other types of animals, especially on the highway. For effect they packed us into it sitting with our heads between our knees. We could not raise our eyes until it was time to get off the truck and go to our specific barracks area somewhere on the post. Suddenly the truck stopped and the door slammed open.

"Get your sorry asses off of my fuckin' truck, you maggots!" I looked into the meanest grey eyes I had ever seen. "You heard me! What the hell are you looking at? Get moving, privates!" We jumped off the truck and ran onto the platform of the starship trying to figure out where we were supposed to be and what to do. The starship was our new home for eight weeks. It was nothing like the reception station. It looked like one of the big buildings in an office park but it definitely was not that. It was a brick-brown, square complex that held four basic training companies, a headquarters in the front and a dining facility in the middle. We were in a staging area within the complex that looked like covered parking. Several drill sergeants--along with the one we would come to know--were standing around screaming commands. "Got dammit, private! What the hell are you doing? Get your ass over there into formation!" It was organized chaos. At first I really wanted to cry but I was so disorientated I forgot about it.

Sweating and breathing hard, we rushed to the place we were supposed to stand. On the way one of the other soldiers bumped into me and knocked my hat off my head. I tripped and fell as I tried to pick up my headgear. A female soldier reached down to help me to my feet. I grabbed her hand and was stunned when I gazed into a kind, beautiful face, with a smile like Gabriel. She was a specialist, which was a higher rank than the rest of us privates, but she was still running around like we were. It was her first day too. Her smile hypnotized me as she helped me to my feet. That interaction did not help the situation.

"Thank you," I said.

"No problem."

"Get your fuckin' sorry asses into formation, NOW! Drop!" We tried to run in the direction the drill sergeant was pointing. "Drop, slug! You don't know what drop means, idiot? Moron, get down and do pushups now! You too!" The drill sergeant was gesturing at somebody. I got down as quickly as I could to start doing pushups. Pain was making me rethink my decision to join the military. Then, I looked over and saw her again. The female who was doing pushups with me was the same one who helped me. I saw that her name was Scott. I think I said her name aloud because she winked at me and made me smile as I pushed. "Oh, you got something to smile about, fly shit? Roll over!" The drill sergeant interrupted my visual. As I did the drills, I thought about the pretty, new friend I got in trouble with. "You sorry sacks of shit! Get up! Get down! Get up!" Now it was time to focus on getting this drill sergeant off my ass. "Get over there and get ready for shake down! Move! I said move, horse shit!" My sister didn't write home about this crap. This was purgatory with a grey-eyed demon spitting fire and calling us all kinds of names.

Anyway, that started hell week. It's ironic that my life ended exactly the same way. I died with people running around, screaming commands.

## Chapter 2

Try the military if you're a masochist. There is a fully trained and highly motivated sadist waiting just for you. We had a dedicated professional assigned to our asses. For the next few weeks, pain, terror, teamwork, training, pain and terror filled our lives. The only things we had to look forward to were chow, personal time, and some portions of Sundays. We quickly learned that going to church alleviated a little torture each week. Some of us were seeking salvation but most of us were trying to get into the safe zone. Service was the best way to avoid our twisted female drill sergeant, Sergeant First Class (SFC) Jones—aka The Jackal. The gargoyles at the entrance wouldn't let her in the church.

You would think she was nice just by looking at her. She was pretty and looked sharp every day. Never was a hair in her perfect ponytail out of place. She had flawless mocha skin, white teeth, meticulously detailed eyebrows, and long eyelashes complimented by those demon grey eyes.

The other morning I walked into her office at the front of the bay. She had her hair down and was wearing a T-shirt and digitized cargo pants. The Jackal had a body like a brick shit house. All muscle and no flab with a nice, tight behind. Even I had to say, "Damn." I wanted to look like my leader but that was it. The bitch had a mental problem. It was hard to see beyond the pain she joyfully inflicted on me daily.

SFC Jones developed a special program of torture for me and a few other privates who went through under her watch. She always put us on her work details, Kitchen Duty, or just plain dogged us. She said we would thank her for it later in our careers. I still have yet to thank her.

One Sunday we were on our way back from service. "I hope you all said your prayers because you are going to need some help from above when I get through with you!" *Damn it!* What has the platoon done now? "Get over here privates and beat your face. Do some push-ups! Doooooowwwwwnnnn…. Up!" SFC Jones counted in a slow cadence designed to cause extra pain. She liked to talk while torturing.

"I see that no matter how many times I tell you trifling sows to G.I. the latrines to standard before you do **ANYTHING ELSE**, you can't seem to get it done! What does it take for you to keep my bay area clean, dirt eaters?" All fifty-eight of us lived on one floor that was an open bay. Our bunks lined up in rows with wall lockers on the bunks' left and right. There was a walkway between the rows of beds. The latrines were at the very end with ten stalls, ten showers and ten sinks. One of the idiots in our platoon left something in the latrines. They should know better by now. Damn them!

"Get your goat smelling asses into my barracks, get into the latrine and clean up your nasty female droppings, now! As a matter of fact, meet me by your bunks!" Just another day with SFC Jones. I guess she did not have anything to do at home, so she came in to dedicate her time and attention to us.

We ran through the staging area upstairs to our bunks. She followed us and smoked us for about an hour, ranting included, and made us clean up the whole latrine for one piece of paper being on the floor. Then she left. "And this shit better look the same way when I get in here in the morning!"

"Yes, Drill Sergeant," the platoon screamed in unison. As soon as our drill sergeant left, many of the girls started crying, but not me. Fuck her! I vowed she would never make me cry. I held mine in just for spite. If the lunatic didn't want me to cry so badly, I probably would have. She walked out and I kept it moving.

"Who does she think she is anyway?" I continued talking shit in my head as I went down to the laundry room to get my things from the dryer. I froze in terror when I saw The Jackal leaving the laundry room as I approached it. I snapped to the position of attention. To my surprise, SFC Jones only stopped and looked at me. Then she scoffed and continued on her way. Relieved, I quickly went inside.

"What's up, kid?" Jeez! I nearly jumped out of my skin. It was Scott and we were alone.

## Don't Ask, Don't Tell

"Hey. You scared the shit out of me, girl!" I replied as I gathered my things. I wasn't trying to stay long. Jones the Jackal might be on her way back.

"Aren't you a trainee leader," she asked.

"No, I'm not."

"What's your name?"

"Um, I'm Dahni. I mean, McPhail." It was on my shirt.

"I've seen you around here," she said. I continued to hurry. "Yeah, we kind of met the first day. You helped me when I fell."

"Right, right. That's where I remember you from." Did she really forget me? I did not forget her.

As Scott continued talking, it dawned on me that she was surprisingly comfortable knowing the Jackal was prowling the area. "Where are you from?" She walked toward me while I rolled my socks, underwear and my T-shirts. She moved close and I got nervous. Why did I get nervous?

"I'm from PA. Right outside of Philly."

"I'm from Maryland." She extended her hand. "It's nice to meet you." I shook her hand and she held on for a few extra seconds. My palm started sweating almost immediately, so I pulled my hand away.

"Nice to meet you too," I said nervously.

"I like your braids. Is it all yours?" She touched my hair.

"Yeah, it's mine." I let my hair grow out so I could keep it in cornrows throughout training.

"How old are you, McPhail?"

"Um, eighteen. You?"

"Twenty six."

"Wow! You're that old? What are you doing here with us?" Twenty-six was shocking because everyone else was my age. "I'm paying off college loans. You got a boyfriend?" She continued the interview.

"You mean at home? Nah, I don't have a boyfriend. Hey, I gotta go before the Jackal comes back. I don't feel like getting my ass smoked again for nothing." I turned to leave.

"Who? Drill Sergeant Jones? She's gone for the day. She's not coming back." Scott seemed very confident in her knowledge and again, *comfortable* when I mentioned the terror of our basic training lives. This, among other things, intrigued me.

"How do you know that she's gone for the day for sure Scott?"

"Oh, I know. Trust me. She's gone. So you don't have a boyfriend?" This chick was starting to weird me out.

## Don't Ask, Don't Tell

"No. Why?" After I answered, she moved very, very close to me. Close enough that I could smell her. She looked me in the eyes with her special power and said, "Can we be friends?"

Nothing. . . The words would not come. What was wrong with me? I wanted to say, "Yeah! Yes, I would love to be your friend!" But then I felt stupid for wanting to be her friend so badly. Weird, even. I reached for my clothes so I could just leave but she grabbed my hand. "Will you be my friend?" Fire coursed through my veins at her touch. I remembered a similar feeling from Sergeant Fitzgerald's kiss. This was more intense.

"Yeah. Um, Yes. Uh. . .Yes, I will." I snatched my hand away and ran from the laundry room. My heart was pounding and not from the earlier exercises either. My heart was pounding because of Scott. I hurried into the open bay, which now seemed very small. Everyone was looking at me. No they weren't. I just felt that way. I sat on my bunk and put away my belongings, I kept thinking about how it felt when Scott touched me. It really was like fire.

As I prepared for the next day, I decided not to think about what happened. It was best to put that out of my mind and bed down. Four-thirty would be coming fast and I wanted to get in as much sleep time as I could. I needed all my energy to deal with the Jackal in the morning.

*

## Dahni McPhail

You have GOT to be kidding me. Bang! Bdadadadaaanng! Ka Pow! Everybody jumped or fell off their bunks as a steel garbage can crashed down the middle of the isle, ripping us from sleep. This kind of bullshit is why I named SFC Jones "The Jackal." Only a demon would think it's a good idea to terrify people like this at four-thirty in the morning.

"Hurry up and get your worthless asses up and out of my barracks, privates! Move, move, move! You better clean up your nasty female droppings or there's going to be trooouuuubbblllee! Get moving! McPhail, beat your face!"

Damn! What did I do in my sleep? Rather than question our insane ruler, I began the day's torture session. She was on a roll and we were on the smash list.

The Jackal walked up and down the aisles of the bay screaming at the top of her lungs. "You are a fucking disgrace to the United States Military. You need to pack your shit and go back home to your Mamas in SHAME! SHAAAAAAME," she roared! "Get up, McPhail!"

"Yes, Drill Sergeant!" I was damn near dead when she remembered I was doing pushups.

The rant continued. "You filthy maggots are an embarrassment to the female species. I do not want you here. I want to send your asses back where you came from! But I will not give you the satisfaction! Squad leaders, get over here!" The half-dressed trainee leaders ran over to SFC Jones and stood at attention. "Guess what? YOU ARE

## Don't Ask, Don't Tell

FUCKIN FIRED! Get those leadership brassards off your shoulders and get your funky, tired, sorry, worthless, asses out of my face!"

OK, The Jackal--at four-thirty a.m.--fired all the appointed leaders. "Benning, since you can't seem to keep these tragic failures in order, YOU'RE FIRED TOO!"

. . .And she fired our Platoon Guide. What was going on? She continued the shock session. "Benson, Dorsey, Howard, Sanders!" They sped to the front where she stood. "You are my new squad leaders. The Jackal threw the brassards at them. "McPhail!" My eyes got as big as saucers. "You are the new platoon guide. Here!" I hadn't made it over to where she stood because I couldn't move. She threw the brassard at me. "Fuck up so I can fire your sorry asses too! Get my bay area cleaned and get out here for formation in five minutes! Four-fifty nine!" The Jackal started the countdown to pain.

She was the definition of disturbed: consistently exhibiting erratic behavior. The Jackal smoked the dog shit out of us yesterday. Then, this morning she came in and put The Kru in leadership positions. Who is *The Kru?* We're the five privates who ran things and kept shit together when our drill sergeant was not around. We kept her off our asses. The other soldiers just started calling us that. We spent all our time together, none of us ever shed a tear since training started, and we were just as hard-core, mean, and physically fit, as our drill sergeant was. We didn't give a fuck what The Jackal did. To us, she was just another unhappy bitch with problems at home.

## Dahni McPhail

In our first few leadership moments, we made sure they cleaned the bay and put the platoon into formation before The Jackal took position out front. This was our first accomplishment. The Jackal came out to the formation and simply said, "Now that's what I'm talking about! McPhail, move them to chow!" The Kru and I looked at each other like, "Hell yeah. Now what?"

"Counter-column, March!" I gave the command; we executed the movement perfectly and went to the dining facility for breakfast. Could life really be getting better for us just like that?

"McPhail, get your ass over here. This is the duty roster for tonight." Our first night as leaders and we had duty. Duty meant less sleep. I was not happy about that shit. We still had to do everything everyone else did, but we had two hours less time. I was already tired just thinking about it. Next The Jackal gave me the day's tasks. "Here's everything that needs to be done before we march out to the rifle range. Don't fuck it up." The Jackal left a list of shit a mile long and walked away.

I immediately pulled The Kru together for a planning session. "OK, y'all. I figured it all out. The Jackal is trying to fuck us over. Look at this shit." I showed them the list. Everyone groaned but Sanders raised up.

"McPhail, fuck that ho! We can do this shit like we always do, man. We ain't got to do it by ourselves. These slugs have to do it. All we have to do is make them do it." Sanders was a former high school basketball star from New York. About five/six, slightly bow-legged with a body that looked like every woman's fantasy. I think she ran point in school. In training, she was my first squad leader. She knew about everything that was going on and that quality made her invaluable.

"Sanders is right, McPhail." Dorsey added. "We can do it." Dorsey was the fourth squad leader. "Let's just split it up. You know what the dumb asses in your squads can do, right?" She looked at us. "OK, we'll divide it by what they won't fuck up and cry about." Then Benson and Howard jumped in and identified what their squads were capable of doing. By the time we went inside the dining facility to eat, we decided who was going to do what, assigned the tasks to the person responsible, put the fear of an ass whooping in the platoon's minds and were ready to rock.

I love it when a plan comes together. We sat down to eat and Benson started laughing. We were like, "What? What's funny?"

"That bitch is going to be mad that we got this shit done! She's going to have to think up some more ways to harass us. You know she wants us to fail." We all agreed. We would stick this out together. While we were bonding and building a strong fortress of friendship in the face of our imagined conspirator. The Jackal wasn't even thinking along those lines.

Ten minutes after chow, we stood ready in formation with all soldiers and gear. "Great job, troops! Get ready to move out. We've got a long day ahead." The Jackal gave us a thumbs-up and walked into the office in front of the staging area. Now The Kru was astounded. The Jackal didn't make us roll on the ground, do push-ups or have us on our backs in the "dying cock-roach" position feeling major pain. We must have been doing something right. Thank goodness. We'd take relief any way we could get it.

## Chapter 3

The day went the same way days usually went. The Jackal was on the rifle range screaming and whacking us upside our Kevlar helmets with her brass rod. One of the privates mistakenly pointed a loaded weapon at the Drill Sergeant and paid dearly with an onslaught of exercises designed to bring blood into the brain for additional focus and functionality. Same shit, different day.

We got back to the barracks after training, cleaned and stored our weapons then got ready for personal time. "Assholes, come here." The Jackal was calling us by our pet name. "Today, you did an outstanding job. It's hard for me to believe myself. Keep up the good work and get ready for duty tonight. Make sure all of your people are briefed and none of them is late. If one person is late, they don't pay. You pay." The first half of the comment sounded like it came from a stranger. The last part came from the one we knew all too well.

Everything was straight with the platoon. We got ready for a long night of security checks, answering phones, waxing floors and all the crap associated with duty. "I'd rather be sleeping," I said.

"You can say that shit again, dog."

"Sanders, who are you on duty with?"

"I'm on duty with somebody from another platoon. I don't even know her." Sanders' observation made me pay attention to the fact that we were not on duty with our own team.

I winced, "Me either. I'm on duty with Scott." Each of us was on duty consecutively but not with each other like we thought we would be. That trashed our sleeping plans because we damn sure weren't going to stay up the whole duty period. When it sunk in that I had duty with Scott, I became especially tense.

I walked up to the headquarters and reported for my shift in nervous anticipation. When I arrived, no one was at the duty desk. I settled in and started studying my Smart Book to prepare for tomorrow's tasks. "What's up, McPhail?" I looked up from my book. It was Scott. Nothing would come out of my mouth. Why did this keep happening to me?

"McPhail, aren't you going to speak?"

"H. . .hi. Hi, Scott."

"What's wrong with you? Do I make you nervous?" Hell yeah.

"No, you don't make me nervous. Why would you?" Even though she did make me nervous, I had to find guts enough to open my mouth and say something unstupid.

"What's up with you, Scott?"

"Nothing. Pissed like everybody else because I have to pull duty." She walked around the counter and entered the cubicle door.

"I see all your home girls are also pulling duty tonight." She sat down next to me. I could hear my heart pounding loudly.

"Yeah, Scott. It's a bunch of bullshit but I'm not about to say anything to our crazy ass drill sergeant. We'll just pull it. Fuck it." I put my book on the counter.

"Did you just turn eighteen?" Scott didn't waste any time starting the interrogation.

"No. Well yeah. A few months ago." I am stupid for no reason around this woman.

"You're still a baby, then."

"Pretty much as far as my parents are concerned. It's my first time away from home like this."

"Are you an only child?"

"No, I'm the youngest. Is there anything else you want to know?"

She laughed. "Am I getting on your nerves?"

"You do ask a lot of questions. I'm just wondering why you all up in mine."

"I'll stop if I'm bothering you, McPhail." *If I had known then, what I know now, I would have told her to stop asking me questions, but instead...*

"I don't mind you asking me questions. People just don't act like you where I come from. They mind theirs. But this is the military and people are different. Ask."

"OK. Have you dated a lot of guys?" Damn. That was a strange question.

"I've dated some guys but I have more friends than dates. I'm not into boys. I'm not trying to get pregnant. I have too much to do in life."

"I hear that," she smiled.

Scott went on and on and freaking on with the questions. She was very interested in what I had to say: my hobbies, my family--everything. She was very interesting too. She told me that she graduated from college with a bachelor's degree in nursing but she joined the military because she didn't want to be saddled with bills from school. The military pays off your college loans and all you have to do is serve a few years. Plus she came in with some rank because of college. She was single with no children and she was just trying to make a better life for herself while in the service. Real smart, pretty, funny and interesting. She smelled good too.

"I have something else to tell you McPhail. I want to be straight up with you and you can decide now whether you want to continue to be my friend or not. I feel that if we are going to be friends, we need to be honest with each other. Do you think you will be able to handle it if I told you some things about my past, McPhail?"

"Um, your past is none of my business unless you killed some people and want me to be your next victim. Anything other than that, I can deal with."

"OK, well I used to date women while I was in college."

"What do you mean, date? Like a guy dates a girl? Are you saying you're a dyke?" Scott's head snapped in my direction. *Well, that was the only word I knew to use. Nobody in my circle of family and friends was a dyke. That's what my friends at home called it.*

"Um, please don't use that word," she said.

"What word, 'dyke?' Scott, you're a fuckin dyke? Why don't you like guys?"

She turned to me again and looked at me like she was going to say something but then she changed her mind. "McPhail, it's a personal preference. I felt this way all my life. Now, I told you this as a friend. If you are going to spread my business all over the place and call me names, you are not the person I thought you were."

"Shit, chick," I exclaimed. You're not the person I thought you were!" She looked at me like I hurt her feelings.

"Scott, I'm just kidding. I'm joking. I don't know anything about your lifestyle, and my parents raised me to be kind toward people and definitely not to tell secrets if someone chooses to confide in me. However, a caveat to our friendship is that I reserve the right to talk shit to yo funny-freaky-ac/dc ass whenever we're alone and I get the opportunity to do it--as long as it's just between us!" I laughed at the funny-freaky thing I said.

"Ha, Ha, McPhail. You are not funny."

"I know I'm not, but you are, Scott!" We both laughed.

"Are you two supposed to be on duty or at fucking comedy hour?" The Jackal arrived. When we had duty, she had duty.

"Drill Sergeant, on duty, Drill Sergeant!"

"Then shut the hell up. Read your smart books. The only talking you need to do is when you answer the phones!"

"Yes, Drill Sergeant!" We started talking again as soon as The Jackal departed the area.

*

In fact, we talked for the entire time we were on duty that night. Scott was cool as a fan. I was glad to find out she was so friendly. I put the fact that she was a dyke to the back of my mind.

"Well McPhail, it was nice talking to you." Our shift was over and the next team arrived with Sanders and some other chick.

"Nice talking to you too." Then, Scott put her arms around me and gave me this full body hug and **Fire!** Fire shot through my veins again. I didn't move or hug her back. Scott pulled away from me and smiled as she walked out the door back to her barracks.

"What the fuck was that, D?"

"Shit, Sanders, you got me. I don't know. I guess she is just a friendly person." I tried to explain the lengthy hug.

"You better tell that bitch you don't have a dick. You got a dick, McPhail?"

"Yeah, Sanders. Suck it. Fuck you and good night." I left the battalion area thinking about what Sanders said. I got in my bunk and closed my eyes to go to sleep. I kept thinking about Sanders asking me if I had a dick. Then I thought that if I had one, I'd stick it in Scott if she let me.

\*

"Lights On!" Get up and get moving, privates!" Wow. This was a change. Maybe I'm not still in this hellhole. There were no trashcans rolling down the aisle. "Get your asses out of my barracks! You got five minutes! Drop, McPhail!" OK, I'm still here.

As we went through the different phases of training, The Jackal got a little less horrible. The torture lessened and the teaching increased. That was a welcomed change. The Kru remained in charge. She hadn't fired us and that in itself was amazing. The Jackal hadn't injured or maimed us and we still had leadership positions. That's because Benson, Sanders, Dorsey, Howard, and I had our shit on lock. We pulled duty constantly but between that and training, we still somehow managed to get everything done. We were functioning like a well-oiled machine. After training one night we were chilling in the break area: an open square within the starship that reminded me of a tiny park because it had little trees and benches. It was an authorized cigarette smoking area but the rest of us could chill there during personal time.

"Hey, y'all. Can I tell you something?"

"Not really, Benson". Sanders was always teasing. We laughed.

"No, for real. I'm for real about this shit." We looked at Benson with a sort of fear thinking that she might tell us she kicked someone's ass and we all were going to be in trouble. Benson was another pretty, crazy chick. Mocha complexion with long brown hair that always looked sun bleached. She kept it in a ponytail. Cool as shit, desirably intelligent and she would fight anybody in a minute. We knew something wrong was about to come out of Benson's mouth. We didn't expect. . . "The girl I was on duty with kissed me in the mouth the other night. She told me not to tell anybody but I can't keep it to myself."

"What the fuck? She kissed you in the mouth? The mouth?" That shit blew us away or so I thought.

Howard topped Benson when she added "Y'all know the chick that I pull duty with a lot? She kisses me too." *Kisses? She kisses???* Then Sanders and Dorsey said the same thing about girls kissing them on duty. All my friends had done went dyke on me! I was the only one who had not let it happen and I let loose on their asses.

"Y'all bunch of fuggin' bull daggers! Homos! How y'all gonna come in the military and just turn into dykes?"

The way they looked at me, I knew that I really struck a nerve, hurt their feelings, and said exactly what they all feared hearing from people who found out. For that reason only, I felt bad. I apologized. "Damn, I didn't know I would offend you, or whatever I just did. But what's up with that shit? What's going on?" We were best friends. I had to be there for them in this time of need. This was some crazy ass shit.

I listened in veiled horror as one by one each of them recounted the situations leading up to their kiss. The stories were pretty much the same. They started out just by talking to them and over time they got closer and closer with the girl. Then a kiss just happened. I was appalled and intrigued to say the least, especially when they started admitting the deep shit. Sanders was like, "Dahni, I have never, ever felt a kiss that felt that good." (My mind went straight to Scott's touch.) Then Benson's thug ass agreed with Sanders. They all felt the same way. None of them had ever felt so good when they kissed a guy. The confessions seemed endless.

Howard said, "I sneak out and kiss her every night. I can't help myself. I try to stop but I still sneak out and meet her in the parking lot behind the dumpster and we kiss."

"I meet Sherry in the day room," Dorsey admitted.

## Don't Ask, Don't Tell

After all the disclosures, I began thinking, "These muthafuggas have been around here kissing girls for days!"

How the fuck can all of them, The Kru—-the finest female trainee leaders in this camp--be in the mix with chicks like this? They can have any guy they want. Sanders is beautiful with a great personality; well, silly really. Howard was one of the sweetest people I'd ever met. She was tall and built thick, had green eyes and wore long braids too. She said she is Creole. Dorsey is strong and quiet, chocolate with some kind of auburn eye color that I'd never seen before. Somebody hooked her cornrows up before she came to training. Me? My family says I'm "high yellow." I have my mother's eyes and wear mini plats like the brat, tied back. All of us had bodies by design, and with the Jackal torturing us daily, we were cut like TA DOW! Hot to death. Why were we being approached by all these chicks? And why are *they* kissing them?

"Well y'all," I said, "Whatever we do, we can't tell anybody this shit and don't get caught with these freaky deaks. We'll probably get a blanket party from the rest of the platoon. The Jackal's crazy ass will think up some special torture for lesbians and include me regardless of whether or not I've done it. They'll put y'all out of the military for it too. We just have to just keep it between us and figure it out between each other." That day we made another pact to keep the secret that could destroy all our reps and our newfound careers. That night, I had duty again with Scott.

## Chapter 4

"Yes, Drill Sergeant!" I got up from my one-millionth push up. I couldn't seem to do anything right in that woman's eyes. I think she just hated me. I know that I, personally, had not done anything to her. Her special torture for me was about the only thing that didn't change for the duration of basic training. I was so glad that the shit was almost over and graduation was right around the corner. Soon I would be gone from this bullshit and I'd be away from this crazy drill sergeant maniac.

I got myself together and headed up to headquarters for duty mad as hell. Yeah, I was pissed off because the chick wouldn't lay off me. Freaking' psycho.

As I walked up to the duty desk, I saw The Jackal outside the front door talking to Scott. That devil sure gets around fast. Scott wasn't even at the position of attention while she was talking to The Jackal. She was standing there talking with her hands on her hips. I presumed that Scott was about to be doing pushups for that shit real soon. I didn't want to be caught looking so I told Howard and friend to brief me before I relieved them from duty.

"What's up, y'all? Anything happen?" I said that knowing as soon as I got back to the bay, Howard--regardless of the hour--was going to reveal how long and how many times she and this freaky trick had been kissing during their shift.

"Nothing spectacular happened. We didn't have to put anything in the duty log."

"Aiight, Howard. You know we go out to the chemical range tomorrow, right. We have to make sure the platoon is completely ready tonight. We won't have time to deal with them forgetting shit and then have The Jackal kicking our asses early in the morning."

"Yes, Platoon Guide! You know we got that shyt, mayun!" Yeah, I really did know that. We were always on top of things.

I glanced through the double glass doors and saw The Jackal grab Scott by her arm. I fearfully watched as Scott pulled away and stormed into the battalion lobby area to report for duty. The Jackal tore into the door behind Scott. "Got dammit, I said drop! Get down and give me ten, fucking specialist!" Scott swung her body around and looked at Drill Sergeant Jones as if she wanted to kill her. Then Scott got down and did her ten pushups. "One, specialist. I didn't count one damn push up. Sound off or I will never say the number two and you'll be on that fuckin floor all night until you puke!" The Jackal was livid!

"One, drill sergeant. Two, drill sergeant. Three drill ser—gant." Scott's voice started to crack. "Four, drill sergeant. Five…" By the time Scott reached the number ten, she was pushing and crying her eyes out. I knew from watching their conversation outside the headquarters that the Jackal was about to do some crazy shit and be in that ass. But what was up with that? Even The Kru didn't fuck with SFC Jones like that. Neva.

"Private McPhail, you can tell this fuckin specialist to recover after I leave the area and not one second before!"

"Yes, Drill Sergeant," I promptly replied.

I watched The Jackal intently as she kicked the side door open and left. I told Scott to get up as soon as it was safe. "She's gone, Scott. Get up. Damn, are you OK? Why were you antagonizing that fool? I can't believe you did that shit. Then above all else, you let The Jackal make you cry. That motherfucker will never get a tear from me. I'll die first." I wasn't helping. Scott stumbled to her feet. Her face was beet red, her eyes were blood shot and tears and snot ran all over the place. She was trembling and crying. That made me change my approach. "Scott, go into the latrine and get yourself together. I got things out here. Do you want me to get someone to pull duty for you on your shift? I can get somebody from my platoon to do it." Scott shook her head "no" and went into the latrine still crying.

"I'll be glad to get away from that bitch," she said.

"You'll be glad?" I shouted after her. "You ain't the only one. I'll be gladder than you ever think you could be. At least when you cry, she leaves you alone. I ain't never gonna cry and that makes the Jackal torture me even longer! Take as much time as you need to square yourself away."

After about fifteen minutes, Scott came back to the duty desk with her eyes all swollen. She'd stopped but you could easily tell that she had been crying. Poor thing.

"You OK?"

"Yeah, I'm fine. I just let old mean and crazy get the best of my emotions today."

"All right. Well, suck that shit up and control it so that crying doesn't happen again. She doesn't deserve any of your tears. Save them for something worthwhile." Scott looked at me and smiled.

Time passed and we were talking, talking, talking again. Well, Scott asked me questions and I answered them again. She was really getting deep that night.

"Have you ever had sex with a guy?"

"Yeah. I've done it. One of my friends had an orgasm and I was trying to have one but it didn't work. So I just quit altogether."

"Have you ever let a guy go down on you?"

"Hell no! That's some nasty shit. If a guy will put his mouth on me, he will do it to somebody else and I won't be eating somebody else's coochie when I kiss the bastard."

Scott looked at me. "So, you're saying that you've never had an orgasm and you have never let anyone go down on you?"

"Yeah. That's what I'm saying." I felt self-conscious.

"Have you ever masturbated?" How many questions was this chick going to ask me? Embarrassing questions.

"No, I don't play with myself. Do you?" The playing with myself thing--that was an outright lie. Oh yes, I played with myself. Especially since that night I read how this girl did it. I tried her technique on myself and something fantastic happened down there. After that, I didn't want or care to have a boyfriend or any other interaction, really. I took care of things. But for this conversation, "No, I don't."

"Well, I do it, McPhail. I have done it on several occasions—even here. It's good."

"Scott, don't ever touch me again. I don't knock you. Do you. Right now, I'm just about graduating and getting the hell out of here and hopefully never seeing The Jackal again as long as I live and breathe."

Scott turned her chair toward me. "Have you ever thought about me, McPhail?"

"What do you mean have I thought about you? You're my friend. You cross my mind." I knew what she meant.

"No, I mean have you thought about me sexually?"

The cat fucking got my tongue again. I prepared myself for the next lie. I think about Scott a lot. Especially before I go to sleep at night. I didn't know why I always thought about how she was so pretty, nice, smart, and funny. I couldn't keep her out of my head. "No. I don't think about you like that, Scott." As I said it, I tried to time how long it took me to answer that question. It seemed like minutes.

"Do you ever think about any girls?"

"No, I don't think about any girls, Scott. Sorry. I'm not secretly dykey. There is this guy I met at service. I think about him a lot. He's really cute." I was lying.

"Oh. OK. So are you thinking about dating him?"

"We *are* dating as much as we can date here. You know how that is. Once I graduate, I will probably get with him afterward if things work out. If not, I will move on to the next man. I'm sure there is a husband and children in my future somewhere."

"Yeah, I'm sure there is. I'm happy for you and I hope that things work for you," Scott said, sounding a little disappointed."

"Thanks. I know they will."

Just as our conversation ended, Benson and her "duty buddy" reported to relieve us. "What up, B?"

"Nuttin', D. Anything happen tonight?"

"Nope, everything was quiet."

"Good, I hope the shit stays that way. Is Crazyass acting like a crazy ass tonight around here?" Benson was talking about The Jackal.

"She was in here earlier trying to smoke the whole universe but she's somewhere regenerating her evil powers right now. I hope she doesn't come and mess with you guys during your shift. I'm out. I need to go get my shit from the laundry room before some ignorant ass takes it out the dryer while it's still wet and I have to hunt them down and beat the hell out of them. You good?"

"Yeah, I'm good, D."

"Aiite. Later." I headed out the side door to go and get my clothes.

My uniforms were dry and no one had messed with them. Oh happy day. The door opened behind me. "I need to get my things too." It was Scott. I nodded at her and finished rolling up my stuff. I felt her looking at me. Scott was just standing there by her dryer looking at me.

"What?" I asked.

"I don't believe you," she said.

# Don't Ask, Don't Tell

"You don't believe what?"

Scott walked right up to me, put her arms around my neck and tried to kiss me in the mouth. "Bitch, are you crazy?" I pushed her off me, kind of... It was not the pushiest push I'd ever pushed in my life. What was wrong with me? Scott reached up again, grabbed my face, pushed me back against the laundry table and kissed me. And kissed me...and kissed me. Her lips were so soft and her tongue was so demanding and inquisitive. She set me on **Fire!** I felt a tingling in my loins. I realized that I had never been kissed before in my life. Not until now. Then, I realized *I was kissing a girl!* This time, I pushed her off me for real. "Stop it. Get off me." I grabbed my things and hauled ass out of the laundry room all the way upstairs to my bunk. The same bunk where for nights I'd dreamed about exactly what just happened a few seconds ago. I sat there. This time, I was reminiscing.

\*

CRASH! BANG! CRASH! CRASH! BANG! New tactics. The Jackal was beating our bed frames with a steel pole. I couldn't say she lacked creativity. I sat up to see what was going on with Lucifer. "McPhail, Benson, Howard, Dorsey, Sanders, get your monkey asses up here right now! No, drop! Get on the floor and low crawl up here! Crawl, you fuckin' maggots! Crawl!"

We were still half-asleep, belly crawling toward the front of the bay. As we crawled, we realized that this mean, evil bitch threw every type of liquid, powder and other available substance on the cold, hard floor and made us crawl through it this early in the morning. Damn her! "The rest of you females, get your shit and get the hell out of my barracks!" *Don't we go to the chemical range today?* My eyes begged the question to my comrades. *Why is she trying to kill only us?*

"Platoon Guide, Squad leaders, obviously I have given you entirely too much freedom and you have taken advantage of my kindness." *Kindness?*

"When were you kind?" we thought.

"You fucking maggots think you know more than this Sergeant First Class in the United States Military? I have more fucking time shitting in the latrine than you have on active duty. Position of attention, move! Front Leaning Rest position, move!" She made us get in the push up position and then stand up and then, "Get down! Get up! Get down! Get up!" She was only starting the torture session.

The Jackal flipped us, ripped us, pushed us, and stacked us off the sides of bunks until we all were barely moving. Just when I saw Benson looking like she was about to say, "Fuck it," and jump on The Jackal's ass, The Jackal ended the smoke session. "Get your fucking sorry, damn-near-fired asses cleaned up. Clean up my barracks and get ready to go to training. You don't eat this morning!" Out the door she went. No tears. We stood and looked at each other truly bewildered. Then, we did just what she told us to do.

We were still in shock when we got to the wooded area that housed the chemical chamber. Finally Sanders spoke. "Was she crazier than usual or was it just me?" We all laughed.

"Hell yeah, she was on some type of other shit today."

"Fa real. Did you see her face?" Howard made the crazy face the Jackal wore earlier.

Then Benson said, "Well, she was about to get fucked up. She must have seen *my* got damn face."

"Oh, B. We knew you were almost there. Trust me. We're all so very happy she left when she did. I was at the point where I would have helped you kick her ass." I was serious.

Dorsey said, "Actually, she seemed like she caught herself. Like she knew she was crossing the line from training to abuse. I'm glad none of us was really hurt." We unpacked our gear and made sure the rest of our platoon was ready for training.

The Chemical Chamber was some scary shit. We were the first platoon designated to go inside so we didn't know what to expect. I mean, we trained up until this point but never with actual gas.

"Hurry up, privates! Get over here so we can get this shit started." We put on our equipment, checked our masks and made sure there were no leaks like we were taught. Then we moved to the gas chamber. It was a square, wooden hut with no windows, one entrance and one exit.

Film covered the dim yellow light in the ceiling. We looked at each other through glass lenses. We could see the fear in each other's eyes as we entered the dark room.

"First rank, step up!" The muffled voice of the trainer rang out in the room. "Shake your head! Turn your heads to the left! Turn your heads to the right! Remove your masks!" *Do what? Remove our masks?* "Get 'em off! Breathe!" As soon as the instructor gave the command "breathe" the first rank started puking. Loads of snot ran from their noses. They dropped their equipment and shit because the gas burned their eyes and made them water. They couldn't see. "Get your shit, privates! Do not leave your equipment or your buddy! It will be worse than this on the battlefield! At least this won't kill you! Get out of here!" The door opened and the instructors pushed the disorientated privates out the door.

Row by row they went until it was our turn. My heart was in my throat when I saw the trainer gave the signal to add more gas. Then a new instructor stepped forward. We were scared like a muthafugga. A familiar voice started giving the commands...

"Shake your fuckin heads maggots!" We looked at each other. Everyone looked the same in the chemical suits but we could tell who she was. We knew that voice anywhere. "Turn your head to the left. Turn your head to the right! Jump up and down! Beat your face! Get up! Get down!" *What the fuck? Nobody else had to do this!* "Remove your masks, you fucking females! GET 'EM OFF!!!!" Her voice roared through her gas filters. We removed our masks. "BREATHE, damn you! Beat your face!"

The bitch done lost her mind! The chemicals were kicking our asses and she was making us *exercise?* "Get up, get down!" Benson started puking all over the place. She was on her knees. Howard was on the floor before her. It was pure madness! "Get your fucking home girls, Platoon guide!" She was talking to me! I couldn't see or breathe. Then I started puking. The trainer opened the door and my other four friends were close enough to stumble out. I dropped my Kevlar and she kicked it. I had to run to the back of the room to get it. Then, The Jackal stood in front of me as I tried to leave. "Beat your face, McPhail! Beat your fuckin' face! Get up! Get down! Crawl! Where's your got damn equipment private? Get your equipment!" The Jackal was screaming. I was fucked up, barely standing and incoherent. I couldn't breathe. All of a sudden, the door slammed open and four crazy privates came rushing in to get me.

"What the fuck are you idiots doing?" The Jackal screamed. The Kru came in without masks and without permission. The Jackal tried to stop them but the other trainer pushed her aside. Those fools--my friends-- pulled me out of the chemical chamber and dragged me to fresh air.

I fell on the ground heaving but my team lifted me to my feet so the oxygen could circulate better in my lungs. Scott came running over to us. "Is McPhail OK?" Before anyone answered, The Jackal was on the scene again. She threw her mask to the ground.

"Let her go! Let her fucking go! You fucking soldiers are finished! You violated a lawful order when you came back in there to get that maggot! Let her go!"

They let me go and I immediately fell to my hands and knees, still suffering from the effects of the chemicals. "Get up, McPhail!" The Jackal started kicking the dirt and sand into my face. "Get up! The rest of you goat-smelling maggots, you get down and do push-ups until your platoon guide can get her sorry ass up! All of you!" They got down and started pushing. Benson started puking again. They all were heaving. The Jackal knew what it would do to them if they were forced to continue to do exercises. "Scott, get your ass away from here!" The Jackal turned her fury toward Scott who quickly went away. "What are you looking at? What the fuck are you looking at, McPhail? Get your sorry ass up!"

I did not know The Jackal's reasons for trying to kill us that day. I did not know what she was going through. What I did know is that my battle buddies risked their asses to come back and save me from whatever The Jackal planned.

How I did it, I don't even know to this day. Shit was spinning and I was dizzy as fuck, but for my friends--and just because--I held that bitch's gaze and I got up. No tears.

## Chapter 5

Despite the psycho's murder attempt, we lived through that day at the chemical training range. None of us even got in trouble. I mean, the gang didn't get in trouble for coming back inside to get me. We were certain that our lives, careers and everything else were over because of our actions that day. But no, nothing happened. We breezed through the rest of training and were in the final phase. Only a few more days left in hell.

Things changed after that day at the chemical chamber. We didn't pull as much duty. We weren't fired but new soldiers were elected so other privates could get some leadership experience. Nobody bothered us anymore, really.

"The Jackal didn't kill us, she just made us stronger." Once again, we sat in the break area talking trash about our insane leader.

"Yeah, Howard. I know that's right. If she taught me nothing else, she taught me what I don't want to be like as a leader." I went on. "I don't use words like "hate," but I hate that bitch."

"Hell yeah, McPhail. Let me see her ass on the street and she's getting fucked up!" Benson's comments continued to revolve around retaliation. Sitting there, I wondered if any of us would ever see The Jackal after graduation and I wondered if we would hate her as much.

"What up, Kru?" Scott and her crew walked up to us. I found it odd that the kissy kissy girls--who always tried to make us do freaky things--were friends with each other. I wondered what they were up to now.

"Yo, what up, Scott?" I greeted her.

"What are you guys doing after you graduate?" asked detective Scott.

"We're fucking leaving, that's what!" All voices combined, without practice.

"No, maggots! On graduation night, we get to go on pass. We have to be back the next morning by seven a.m. to catch our transportation to the next duty station. Graduation night we can party. So, what are you guys going to do?"

We hadn't thought of anything close to partying because we were so focused on getting the hell out of dodge as soon as we were legally and physically able. Then here come these chicks talking about hanging out. We had no idea what to do.

"Well, we rented the penthouse suite in the Ritz right outside of post. You guys can come. We're going to have some drinks and some food. Nothing too wild. Just hanging out away from all this madness." Scott dropped the information like it was totally unimportant to her. I looked at my buddies and they looked at me. I didn't know what to say. Part of me was trying to figure out how they even knew anything about "off post." Shit, we'd never been off post since we got here or knew anything about it--not even Sanders. These chicks were dangerous.

"Can we get back to you on that? We haven't really thought about it."

Scott's face told me she did not expect that answer. "Yeah, but let us know soon, please. We don't want to buy too much and y'all don't show up."

"Well, I'm sure there are going to be more people there than just us. Why are your purchases dependent on if we come or not? And while I'm asking questions, how did you know how to hook all this up and y'all are right here in training with us? I don't get it." I looked at them suspiciously. I heard before that dykes were sneaky.

"Oh, I'm from around here. Didn't I tell you that?"

"No, Scott. You failed to mention that piece of information." I continued to eye her but abandoned my negative thoughts. She lived here. The whole thing didn't seem as suspicious anymore.

"Yeah, I grew up in this city so I know what's up. I won't let anything happen to you guys and we'll make it back on time the next morning to get our tickets without any problems. At least we'll have one party under our belts to show for all the pain we've gone through here. So, is The Kru in?" Scott was selling it like she wanted a certain answer.

"Well, B, Howard, D, Sanders? Y'all wanna ride out?" I asked.

"Let's do it. We ain't doing anything else." They were in.

"Hey, for real, how are we going to get there and back? We don't have cars here. I'm not trying to be late just to have The Jackal fucking kick me out of the military over some dumb shit. You know The Jackal hates us. What's the plan?" I needed to know.

"Taxi, Dahni." Scott called me by my *first* name for the *first* time. It just rolled off her lips. Dahni. . . Dahni. . .

"Dahni! Damn! Are you deaf?" Sanders was all in my ear.

"Fuck you, Sanders. I'm with it." I guess I drifted away on Scott's voice.

## Don't Ask, Don't Tell

"Listen we're gonna. . ."

So began the graduation night plan starring The Kru and the freaky deaky chicks. It was the beginning of the rest of our lives as lesbians. We didn't know it. We were too stupid, naïve and trusting to even suspect it.

*

As if she hadn't had her fill of causing us severe pain and agony the last eight weeks, The Jackal came up to the bay area for one final round of torture. "Listen up you females! Just because you're graduating today doesn't make you a soldier in my fuckin military. You're still a stinking piece of giraffe shit! Don't you ever forget that you are lower than the belly of a snake in my eyes and you will never amount to shit as long as you draw breath on this earth!"

"With that being said, somehow you imbeciles have managed to win first place in all areas tested. This means that you are Honor Platoon!" She said it and afterward, she smiled. My hatred made me look past how cute she was. I didn't even react to the great news she delivered but the platoon shook our bay area with cheers and celebration.

There was more. "McPhail, Benson, Dorsey, Sanders and Howard, front and center!" Here it comes. We're ready for her bullshit, even today. "You soldiers--she said soldiers--have been outstanding leaders, trainers, and mentors to the rest of the platoon. Even after your leadership stint, you still went above and beyond to help the team. For that, I am promoting all of you and giving you all an award.

Mommy sometimes said, "You could have bought me for a penny," when things were super unbelievable. I felt that way. None of us could even be happy. The shock was too great. We thanked her. Then we went back to our bunks and finished cleaning and packing so we could graduate and leave. We wanted to catch the next thing headed to the Ritz.

And that's exactly what we did. "Remember, no civilian clothes or your ass is mine!" She screamed after us. We changed clothes in the taxi. We didn't give a fuck. By the time the taxi pulled into the hotel, we were fly and our military clothes were tucked safely away in our gym bags. It was time to get it started. We just knew a gang of people was going to be at the party. That's what the freaky girls said.

We didn't see anyone who even looked like they were military privates at the entrance. Everyone looked like money. Oh well, even better. We went inside and asked for directions to the suite. True to their word, they rented the penthouse, presidential, most expensive suite in the place. When the elevator doors slid open, we were in awe.

"McPhail, this shit is bad as hell!"

"Shit, who are you telling? Are you sure we're in the right place? We're gonna get arrested."

"I know, right." We couldn't stop talking about how great the place looked. The elevator opened up to a grand foyer with white marble tiled floors, a chandelier on the ceiling, and beautiful artwork. I touched the wallpaper and I felt the design. There were several different shades of crème, gray and blue. This lead into a spacious living room with wooden floors, furnished with an elegant sofa set. There was a kitchenette with a full bar set-up in front of large windows with a panoramic view of the city. Man, please. This spot was tight.

"You're in the right place" We were astonished as five--count 'em-- five women we barely recognized strutted into the foyer where we stood. We didn't know how to feel or what to do. I mean, what *do* you do in this situation? It's not like we were there on a date but it did seem like they were directing their sexiness toward us. Damn, I said they were sexy. What was I thinking?

My friends and I looked at each other with the same expression on our faces. The look was like "these women are fine." Then my look turned into "What are we thinking?" It was a girl on girl situation to the max. We were confused as shit. I was, anyway. Then a thought popped into my head. "Y'all, I guess the guys will get here later. It's still early."

They all stammered or coughed out a "Yeah. Oh yeah, McPhail. Later."

"Come on in." We walked through the expensively decorated foyer and they guided us through to the other room. The party room. It was bigger and better with a huge flat panel TV, lots of seating and a nice marble and glass table. The table against the wall displayed an assortment of mini quesadillas, barbeque and teriyaki chicken wings, antipasto, small chicken kabob skewers, and shrimp cocktail among other things I didn't quite recognize, highlighted by pretty glasses for drinks. Behind the glasses was the largest selection of alcohol I had ever seen in my life. "Get something to eat, guys." We were starving so we dove into the food and tore it to shreds. "You guys want to watch a movie or listen to some music?" A movie? At a party? What kind of party was this?

Time passed. Benson said, "Um, is anyone else coming? I thought you guys were throwing the killer party."

"Trust, Benson," one of the girls said. "This party is going to be all that. Come and play this game with us."

"What game?" Her answer would start the life changing events.

"It's a little drinking game. It's called 'up the river, down the river.' It's easy. First you. . ." Sherry explained the game to everyone. It did sound easy. Easy to win. We decided to play because we thought that we could beat those chicks and get a laugh while they were drunk. Things, however, did not go as we planned.

"Drink, McPhail!" Scott said. "Oh shit!" This was my fourth shot and I was not an experienced drinker. I could not hang. Everyone else already took at least three shots. They weren't drinkers either. We were getting fucked up fast. "I can't play anymore, guys. I never drank like this before in my life." I had to admit defeat.

"Well let's play some strip poker." *What the hell?*

"For what?" I screamed. "There's only girls in here! Right, Dorsey?"

## Don't Ask, Don't Tell

"Right. We all have the same thing. What are we stripping for? It ain't anything we haven't seen in the showers or in the bay area."

"Tell me about it." This party was getting stranger and stranger and I was drunk and paranoid.

"Well let's play dirty hearts." Scott chimed in. None of us ever played that game before either and we told her. "Don't worry, it's easy. It's a drinking game, but you get a choice." Scott explained that you deal the cards face up to each person. You get a heart, you take a dare, answer a question, or drink. That seemed easy enough. We all decided to play.

Scott called all her little group together while we were shuffling the cards. Sanders said, "Don't be trying to gang up on us and win, damn ya!" The girls laughed.

"We're not. It's not even that kind of game. We're just trying to make sure we watch y'alls lying and cheating asses." We laughed then.

"Yeah, but we're not over there in a football huddle discussing the next play, though. Are we?" We all laughed.

"Sanders, you're crazy."

The game started and the first person who got a heart just happened to be Sanders. Sanders opted for a question. "Have you ever kissed a girl?" Sanders looked at us and we looked at her. We could not help her at all. The Kru all knew that Sanders had kissed the bitch who asked her the question.  Sanders chose to drink instead of answer.  This wasn't going to be so easy either.

The shots went around the table freely.  To me, it seemed like me and my friends were the only ones who received hearts and invasive questions.  Howard got another heart and was like, "Fuck it.  I'll take a dare!"  We all looked at her as if she lost her mind.  "I can't drink no more.  I just have to take a dare.  I'm fucked up."

Scott, the mistress of ceremonies for the night took over.  "OK, Howard.  I dare you to kiss Sherry for ten seconds."

"Aw, hell naw!  Nope, nope, nope, nope!"  Howard had kissed Sherry many, many times before but just not with anyone knowing or watching.  I mean, knowing at the time she did it because she always told us afterward.

"Well, drink then, Howard."  Scott was enjoying her role as ringmaster, getting everybody fucked up and orchestrating shit.

Then Sherry said, "What?  You don't want to kiss me?"  Howard got a look on her face like, "If this chick doesn't shut up. . ."  I guess Howard thought about the drink or the kiss.  Being able to function in the morning or not being able.  Howard chose the kiss.  She kissed Sherry for the whole ten seconds.  *"Let the games begin!"* I heard a voice inside my head saying that shit like an Olympics announcer.

## Don't Ask, Don't Tell

It was my turn. I got a heart next and of course, I was drunk as shit and not willing to drink anymore. I took my chances on a dare. As I said the word "dare," I looked around and realized that everyone was still at the table but somehow they'd gotten all coupled up. "I'll take a dare." I was drunk but feeling safe and secure that knowing how I felt about being and staying straight, none of my friends would say. . .

"I dare you to tongue kiss Scott." I glared at Benson as the words left her mouth. I thought Benson was my friend. How could she do this to me? "Well, McPhail? Kiss her or drink more." The thought of being hung over, dealing with The Jackal while being hung over, and being late getting back to the barracks drove my decision (yeah, right). I closed my eyes and kissed Scott.

*

"Well, damn. I don't want to kiss you if you have to do your face like that!" What was she talking about? "You look like someone asked you to kiss a dog's ass, McPhail. Fuck it. Don't kiss me. I quit and I'm going to bed. Good night all. Sherry, don't let them forget to set their alarms." I guessed the "party" was over.

Scott stormed out of the room and I sat there and looked at everybody as they were looking at me. "McPhail, that was fucked up."

"What was fucked up, Dorsey? That I had a problem with tongue kissing a girl, you faggot. Shit, I'm straight. Yeah, I had a problem with it. I don't knock anyone else. This is me. I had an issue with the whole thing."

"Alright, Dahni. Damn. We understand. But you didn't have to be fucked up about it. That's all we're saying," Dorsey reasoned.

"Yes I did have to be fucked up about it." Inwardly, I felt bad about it and guilty because I wanted to do it. I had to keep up my front. I got up and went to the table to get some more food so I could eat my high down. It seemed like it was late but as late as I thought it was, it was only about 10:30. That was a relief. I could come down from my buzz, go to sleep, get up and be on my way. Fuck da Lesbos and my newly lesbianated friends for now.

I put in an action movie and watched it. After a while, I started getting kind of sleepy. Two by two, my friends disappeared with the girls. Eventually I was alone so I decided to turn in. I grabbed my bag and went into the bathroom to clean up and brush my teeth. I looked into the adjacent room and saw Scott lying on the bed. After I finished my hygiene regimen, I went and sat on the bed next to her.

"What up, Scott."

"Dahni, you're an asshole that's what's up."

"I'm an asshole because I don't want to kiss your lesbian freaky ass? I told you I was seeing someone. You shouldn't have even played me like that."

"You decided to play the game, McPhail. Nobody forced you to."

"Right and I reacted the way that I reacted. I'm sorry if it came out the wrong way or you took it to heart. Did I mess up your plans?" I started laughing because I was intentionally being a smart ass but Scott was serious.

"Everything is not a joke, McPhail"

"I know. I apologize for my intolerant behavior. Do you forgive me?" I gave her my "forgive me" look. Scott turned and looked at me, then smiled that beautiful smile.

"Don't do that, she said."

"Do what, Specialist Scott? Sealyn. What am I doing now?"

"Don't give me that look."

"Girl, you're obviously delirious. How much did you drink?" I lay down on the bed next to her. I was coming down from my buzz and getting sleepy.

"Where am I supposed to sleep, Scott?"

"You can sleep here with me or sleep on the couch. It's a pull out."

"Do you mind if I sleep in here with you with my attitude?" I was teasing her again.

"No. I don't mind."

"Scott, tell me something about you that I don't know," I said.

That question opened the door for a deep conversation. Scott told me about herself before. Tonight's conversation was new and improved. She told me about being in a relationship and coming in the military trying to get away from her lover because her lover had a screw loose. Her girlfriend was violently jealous. "Damn, so women fight women too? What the fuck? You would think they'd be able to do better in relationships."

"Yeah. You would think that, Dahni. That's not the case many times. Women have more bullshit going on than men ever would. Nevertheless, attraction is attraction. If women are what you prefer then you have to deal with all the shit that comes with loving a woman and her complicated mind."

I was lying on my side looking at Scott's face when I asked, "So, are you free from your girlfriend now? Are you single?" Why was I asking her that?

"Me and my girlfriend are no longer together in my mind."

I thought Scott was finished talking about it, but she went on to tell me about some of the bullshit she went through with her x-girlfriend. That bitch was insane. "And just when I thought I was away from her, she showed up again."

## Don't Ask, Don't Tell

"Why didn't you just fuck that mutha fugga up?" I couldn't grasp letting a female pound on me.

"Because she's crazy and I can't beat crazy, that's why. The more violent you get, the more violent she gets. It's a lose/lose situation. I truly think things could have escalated to me being hurt or killed. She almost broke my arm once." Scott's voice cracked. "I was begging her to please leave. She was accusing me of cheating on her but I wasn't. It was while I was in school trying to finish my degree. She thought I was sleeping with my professor. So, she beat me senseless and put my arm in some type of combat hold."

"Hold up! Your ex is in the military?"

"Yes."

"Where?"

"In Texas. Anyway, that night it really hit home that there was no way out but by ambulance or coroner. I went to see the recruiter the next day."

Scott started sobbing. *What does a person do in this situation?* My sisters always hug me if I cry. So, I pulled Scott close to me and hugged her—completely forgetting about the fire that would erupt in me. How could I forget about that thing that happened whenever I touched her? "That's some fucked up shit for anybody to have to go through. I'm sorry you had to go through that." Nice Dahni had entered the building.

"Thanks, McPhail."

"No problem." I reached over her and turned off the light. When I moved back into my previous position, I was face to face with Scott. Breathing her air. I lay still.

But Scott didn't. She reached toward me and pulled my lips to hers. I made a feeble attempt to pull back but her tongue lulled me into submission. She slid her warm tongue into my mouth while her lips pressed against mine. I was going crazy on the inside. I mean, I just didn't know what to do. So, I kissed her back. I slid my tongue into her mouth and the woman took my tongue and started sucking it. That was new. I was definitely out of my league. Dazed, confused and throbbing, I pulled back.

But she followed me. She moved with me and slid her body on top of mine while she continued kissing me. She reached and grabbed my hands and put them on her waist. Nervously, I started moving my hands over her body. She was so sexy; so pretty and so freaky. I touched her in places that I knew I really shouldn't have. She was still kissing me. Tonguing me. She stopped kissing my mouth. After a brief moment, I quivered when I felt the sensation of her lips on my neck. A searing flame went through every part of my body as soon as I felt her lips doing their work. She was kissing, sucking and tonguing my neck. It all was so very hot. Scorching. She knew exactly where to put her mouth to make me go crazy. I wanted to stop her, but I couldn't. It felt so good. Seriously.

## Don't Ask, Don't Tell

Just when I thought that things could not possibly feel any better, she started a trail of kisses down to my chest. She skillfully pulled my wife beater over my head and placed her lips on my nipple. That's when I really thought that I was going to scream. The previous fumbling of What's-his-name didn't even compare to this woman's ability. I was so turned on by her touch that I was shaking. Everything she did felt good. I never imagined--in my life--something being so hot and so scary and so good all at one time. She didn't give me time to think. She was all over me in a smooth and non-pressuring type of way. Sealyn was confident and quite cool as she moved her mouth over my nipples, exciting them. I felt myself arching against her. Pushing myself toward her mouth.

She spread my legs open, then slid in between my legs and started moving her body against mine. The whole time, she never stopped tantalizing me with her mouth. I was so amazed that a girl could make me feel that good. My body told her I wanted whatever she was going to do to me next.

She obliged. After a trail of kisses that led to my navel, I felt her pulling down my panties. Just the act of her pulling them down over my hips had me completely turned on. Her lips still worked me, kissing my stomach, my pleasure region, my mound, and my thighs. . .crevices. Then she opened my legs wide and changed my life forever.

Sealyn put her mouth on my clit and ruined any man's chance of being in my life in the future. *What is she doing to me?* "It's OK. I've got you. Just relax." *Did I say that out loud?* This woman was really driving me crazy. She kept licking me and gently sucking me. Her tongue had magic powers. Everywhere it touched, I lost yet another part of my mind. I didn't know what I was doing. I was making noises and grabbing and. . . It was wild. Once more, when I thought that things could not get any hotter, she slid her fingers inside me. Damn.

I slightly remember the things that happened after that. What I can recall--in between me losing the last portion of my mind--was Sealyn's tongue continuously licking me while her hot fingers of fire simultaneously went in and out of my area of awakening. I was being fucked by a girl. Oh, this was one hundred percent fucking regardless of what I'd known to be fucking before this scenario. She had me screaming and near tears. I mean screaming, moaning loud, whatever you want to call it. She was changing my perception of life. Never did I think. . . Who knew that a woman could?

Sealyn locked my leg inside her arm and put me in a position where I could do nothing but receive everything she was doing to me. Then, for what seemed like eternity, she made a type of love to my body that I'd never felt before and have only wanted since. Sealyn made love to me that night until I begged her to stop, but she didn't stop. I trembled and came for the first time in my life. Then she made it happen again and again.

## Chapter 6

The Kru was very quiet on the ride back to the training compound. We all just looked at each other waiting for one of us to start the conversation. I was kind of looking at them and then not looking at them, inwardly wondering if they heard what happened in my room. I was embarrassed from the time Sealyn woke me up.

"Dahni, sleepy head. We have to get back to the B's by zero seven hundred. Its six now." I woke up naked and ashamed. "Get up, baby." Sealyn crawled across the bed to me and kissed me on the lips. I just sat there. "Are you OK, Dahni?"

"Sealyn, no. Yes. Maybe. Whatever is the right answer right now for something like this." I got up and walked into the bathroom to shower. She followed me.

"Are you mad?"

"Nah. I ain't mad. I don't know what to feel really. Just let me get dressed. I'll talk with you about it later."

That was the last thing I said to Sealyn Scott for a while. A part of me wanted to pack her in my bags and take her with me. A part of me wanted to get as far away from her as was humanly possible. As my friends and I rode back to the barracks, the newly lesbianated Kru looked and probably felt the same way that I did about the situation. We all were "deflowered" that night. When I look back on it, they set us up. It was more evident when we told each other about our individual scenarios. They played out the same way.

We got back to the barracks around quarter till and got our shit downstairs to make formation. All five of us were going to different places because we had different military occupational specialties. After formation, we went to chow together for the last time.

"McPhail, was it that good?"

"What?" *They heard me!* "What? Fuck you Sanders!" They all just busted out laughing uncontrollably. The shit wasn't funny.

"For real. Was it that good to you? Cause it was that good to me." Howard, Dorsey and Benson nodded in agreement.

"You mean, y'all did it too?"

"Well, we know you did, Dahni!"

"Benson, fuck you!"

"Oh I think Scott already did that!" They started laughing again. We were some sick-n-da-head asses. A life changing event and all we could do was laugh at each other.

"Are you going to do it again?" Dorsey asked quietly.

"I am."

"I am too."

"Yeah."

"Yepper!" They all agreed.

"I don't know," was my response. "I don't know guys. I feel strange. I feel guilt."

"Shit, I'm looking for the next chick right now!" Sanders was always so ambitious.

"Right! Hell yeah." Why are my newly lesbianated friends already talking about being play boi's? I was sitting there torn to shreds and confused and they were already planning the next piece of ass.

"You fools were made for this shit. My heart aches or something is wrong with me." I played with my food.

"Well damn Dahni, it's not as if you're supposed to take this seriously. This is just a way to have some fun and not get pregnant. Then when you meet the guy you want to marry, you just stop."

"Howard, you have the whole thing worked out, huh?" She was full of great ideas.

"Sure do. This will just be one of those things in my past." They went on and on and I listened. I agreed with them that this was supposed to remain a secret. Most definitely that. No argument from me there. I just didn't understand how they took this shit so lightly.

We said our good byes and promised to stay in touch as we boarded the different busses taking us to the next level of training. I was the last of The Kru to leave. I turned to take one last look at the hellhole that imprisoned me for the last eight weeks. I'd never forget all the shit that happened in that basic training complex. I turned to climb aboard and noticed The Jackal standing there watching me leave. Her presence made me hurry up and get my ass on the bus. *Good riddance, bitch!* I thought as loudly as I could. *If I never, eva see your face again in this life or the next, it will be too soon.* I felt an overwhelming sense of relief as the bus pulled away. I leaned back in my chair ready for peaceful sleep.

"So you're not going to talk to me, asshole?" The woman had a knack for scaring the shit out of me. It was Sealyn . I didn't see her get on my bus. I opened my eyes and looked into her beautiful, caramel face. *What are you thinking, Dahni?*

## Don't Ask, Don't Tell

"Um...yeah. I'm going to talk to you. Not here, though."

"Dahni, you haven't said one single word to me. You're just ignoring me and acting like an ass." Why does she always think I'm acting an ass? Just because I didn't jump into her arms after last night and just because I don't know what to say to her. I'm not a lesbian. I don't know what she thinks is going to happen. I just wanted to forget. Plus, I didn't want anyone on this bus hearing what she wanted to say to me. Fuck that. "Is someone sitting here, McPhail?"

"Yes," I lied. I just didn't want her to sit next to me. One, because my heart was pounding and I was nervous and wanted to kiss her, and two, because I thought other people could see on my face what happened between us. "Someone is sitting here." I pulled my bag into the seat next to me and chilled for the ride. Sealyn sucked her teeth and went to another seat.

It didn't take very long to get to the location for our job training. Maybe about three hours. I stayed in my seat for almost the entire ride. When I did get up to use the bathroom, I quickly glanced at Sealyn. She was burning holes through me with her eyes.

The bus arrived at Fort Goodwing and we were called off by our job specialty. Scott's group got off first. As she passed me, she dropped a note on my lap. I hurriedly snatched it up so no one would notice. I was so paranoid. By the time they called my group off the bus, Scott's group was gone.

Our new drill sergeants led us up to our rooms and gave us some time to change our clothes and get ready to come out to formation. Yeah, this was definitely a new environment. The Jackal would have had us rolling down a hill in our dress uniforms, not giving a fuck.

I changed uniforms and set up my wall locker. I had a little while left before formation so I sat down and read the note that Sealyn gave me. It read:

> *"Dahni. I am so sorry if you feel that what I did was wrong. Especially if you are feeling guilty or ashamed. I'm sorry that I was so aggressive and I didn't stop when you asked me to. I know that it was your first time and maybe I should have held back. But I have been feeling you since the first day. I know you plan to move on and marry your friend some day but all I'm asking you to do is not be mad at me. I/we did not set you guys up. We just wanted to spend some time alone with y'all. That's all. I just wanted to spend some time with you. I really am so sorry and I really do care a lot about you Dahni. The fact that you won't speak to me is breaking my heart. Please forgive me. Sealyn."*

I read her letter a few more times and committed it to memory before I tore it into tiny little pieces and flushed it down the toilet. I didn't want anyone to ever, ever find it. Some part of me felt a little better. I don't know if it was because she apologized for taking advantage of my not-so-unwilling ass or if it was because she told me that she actually cared about me. In my heart, I wanted her to care about me and not consider me a notch on her belt. I felt better.

## Don't Ask, Don't Tell

I gathered my notebook and headed downstairs to formation. "PFC McPhail!" somebody screamed. OK now, I know I don't know anybody here at all. Who was this calling my name? "Dahni McPhail?" I turned around.

"Yes?"

"Don't you remember me? Don't you live near Philly? You go to 1$^{st}$ Baptist Church on 7$^{th}$ Street?" *Who was this with all my credentials?*

"Yeah."

"I can't believe you don't remember me!" She did look familiar. She was cute as hell, I knew that. *Dahni, do you hear yourself talking about her as if you're a man?*

"I'm Peaches, girl. I was a year ahead of you. I left and went to college." I thought about it for a second, and then I remembered her. She was the first girl to invade my private thoughts. She looked even better now than she did then.

"Oh yeah, what's up girl? I remember you. You look different. Older or something." *Sexy.* "How did you end up here?" Peaches told me she was in college but she joined the military this summer to pay college bills, of course.

"Peaches, I was just thinking about my friends from basic and how much I miss them. I'm glad we're here together. I feel better seeing you."

"I'm glad to see you too, Dahni. I don't know anybody either."

"Bet, Peaches. When we get back upstairs, we're switching rooms so we can be roommates. Let's get out here to formation now. Don't want to be late for the first one."

We walked out to the formation laughing, smiling and talking. After formation was over, we headed upstairs to switch rooms. Things were going to be OK.

*

Although we were not under the torturous and fear filled watch of The Jackal, our studies were stressful. It's true that the military training prepares you. School was no joke and our curriculum was designed to get us ready to do our real jobs. This shit required a person to pay attention. I barely had time to think about Sealyn.

Lies. That's what I told myself to make my stomach stop hurting. I thought about her constantly. I hadn't seen her or heard from her since we got here and I was wondering where Sealyn's dorm was located. I needed to talk with her and at least apologize. She remained the top subject on my mind, but I spent all my real life free time studying or with Peaches. Last week, Peaches and I met these two dudes from the class next to ours. They were constantly trying to hook up but there just wasn't much time or desire--on my part--for anything except studying, details and class. That's what I told myself.

### Don't Ask, Don't Tell

"Dahnay!" Peaches yelled across the break yard. "Come here, girl!" I went to see why this woman was screaming. "Did you know that we can go to the bowling alley on the weekends after we get finished with our duties?" My eyes popped open.

"I thought we couldn't go during this phase. I thought we didn't get passes until next phase."

"Wrong answer, partna! We could have been going from day one!" Peaches beamed because of the newfound information she got from the guy she was talking to.

"Sounds like a plan to me, Peaches. I know I need to see something different. Why didn't we know this all along? We have to be more inquisitive."

"I know that's right." I mentally decided to find out everything we could do at our new training station. Maybe I'd run across Sealyn if I was out more.

Saturday came and so did Saturday afternoon. They released us for our "on-post pass." This meant that we could go anywhere on post that our feet, the shuttle bus, or a taxi would take us. Peaches and I had to do some personal shopping so we went to the PX store to get toiletries and all that. We left there, got some fast food, and headed to the bowling alley with our goods in hand. There was no way we'd go back to the dorms and risk catching duty. We weren't planning to waste a minute of our limited time.

When we entered, it was packed with people. "Dahni, I guess this is the spot, huh?" We sat down with the two guys we knew and got ready to bowl. We had a great time. Peaches was having a serious conversation with her friend. I engaged in idle chitchat. I didn't want this dude to get any mixed signals. My focus was school.

Before we knew it, it was time to leave and get back to our units. "Time really does fly when you're having fun," Peaches moaned.

"Yeah."

We said goodbye to the guys and were walking away when Peaches' friend asked, "Why aren't you guys going to the club?"

"The club?" Peaches and I looked at each other. "We're not allowed to go to the club."

"You have a pass, don't you?"

"Yeah." Peaches and I kept answering each question at the same time.

"Look at your pass." Well, I'll be damned. I guess reading *is* fundamental. Our passes said that we didn't have to be back until one in the morning if the block was checked. OUR BLOCK WAS CHECKED!

"Damn, Rob. You might just be worth keeping around," Peaches said.

## Don't Ask, Don't Tell

"I hope so," Rob said smiling coyly at Peaches.

"Peaches, you know that dude is trying to get some ass, right? I hope you ain't confused about his strategic kindness."

"I know Dahni. What happens here stays here. I'm not trying to get married."

I raised my eybrow. "You like him?"

"Not really, but he seems to know a lot. I'll keep him as a friend. I hope I'll meet someone I really like AT DA CLUB! We're going to the club!" We started hi-fiving and giving each other dap. We hadn't been out in. . .Well, I'd never gone to a real club come to think of it. So, I was extra happy. I couldn't wait to go to something other than a dance with sponsors.

We made sure the taxi waited for us and dropped our bags off in our rooms. We made up our faces as much as we could and ran out to catch our ride. Earlier, we thought the bowling alley was hot. That was lightweight. The club was huge, loud and dark with flashing lights. The DJ was spinning and the place was packed with people in uniforms. A little different from what I thought of as the normal club, but it was a club all the same and it was crunk! We got on the floor as soon as we hit the door. "There are some fine ass women in here. Damn!"

"What did you say, Dahni?" Peaches could barely hear me over the music. I was glad about that because she would have tripped on what just came out of my mouth.

"I said there are some cuties up in here. Time to get some phone numbers!"

We mixed and mingled around, but always stayed together. We made many new acquaintances and had a ball. "Shit, I wish we could at least get one drink, Peaches."

"Right."

"But there is no alcohol for sale here. We're not supposed to have it." Peaches smiled at me.

"True, however, there are those of us who. . ." She pulled out a couple of small bottles of Patron. "Know how to sneak and get shit, dawg!" At that moment, I decided I loved Peaches. She was all you could ask for or even expect in a friend.

Peaches had three shots for us both. She's the true definition of a baller. I was with the woman all day and didn't see her get the alcohol. But right about now Whoooooo caaaaaaaarrrreeeeeddd? We were fucked up and partying our asses off. "Girl, let me run to the bathroom right quick. I gotta pee."

"I'll go with you, Dahni. I need to use it too." We both went in. Peaches got the first open stall. I had to wait, but not long. I was relieved to see a bathroom door open because I really had to go. The door opened wider and out came Sealyn. I nearly wet my pants.

"Hey, Dahni." She walked around me to the sinks.

"What's up, Sealyn!" I was all smiles. "What are you doing here?"

"The same thing you're doing here. Taking a break and having some fun. I guess you never got around to getting in touch with me, huh McPhail." She was looking in the mirror at me as she washed her hands. What I wanted to say was, "I really miss you and I didn't know how to find you. I don't know where your building is." But, I didn't.

"You know how school is, Scott," is all I said.

"No, Dahni. I know how *you* are. You're such an ass." Sealyn started walking out the bathroom door and I was about to let her go.

I finally said, "Wait. Where are you?" She rolled her eyes up in her head.

"Why?"

"Just tell me where you are, Sealyn."

"I'll tell you what, McPhail. I'll get back to you about where I am just like you got back with me about our conversation. Bye, asshole."

She turned away from me and walked out the bathroom door. I stood there watching the door close. Why was she acting like this? I told her I was busy with school. I'm sure she was busy too. Why was she angry with me? "Who was that, Dahni? Peaches caught the tail end of my interaction with Sealyn.

"She's someone I know from basic."

"I know her. Well, I've seen her before. She's in Rob's school." I turned and looked at Peaches. If I thought she wouldn't have tried to kiss me back, I would have hugged her and kissed her! Damn, that woman was useful! Sealyn was in Rob's school!

## Chapter 7

It was Wednesday. Peaches and I were already planning the weekend ahead. We both had high averages in school, which was great because our grades and our behavior assured our "off-post passes" for the weekend. Off post, baby!

"Dahni, I went on the internet and booked us a room at the Colonial. That's where all the permanent party guys go. It's a nice spot with lots of parties. We'll just split the cost between us."

"Aiite. We got a room for both nights?"

"Yeah."

"Cool. Can you think of anything that will interfere with us being released Friday after class, Peaches?"

"Nope. Not unless these other morons do some dumb shit and we get mass punishment. If everybody stays out of trouble, things will be fine, D."

Things were fine. Friday at 7 p.m., we were in a Taxi and on our way to our hotel room. We arrived and checked into our room. It was nothing like the other spot but it was still nice enough to chill out and party in though. Peaches was determined to get some unconditional and casual sex this weekend. "The best ones to mess with are the permanent party guys because they won't come looking for you every weekend. They just hit it and go." I was listening to her instructions, but I was more interested in going to the parties happening in the hotel. I didn't want the male/female hump situation. I just wanted to have some fun!

Fun was not the word to describe what I was having. There literally was a party in every room except ours and I was in every room except ours. Everybody had drinks and food. Some people were doing drugs but that's never been my thing. I was just walking around drunk as shit and dancing up on asses. It didn't matter which gender the ass was and they didn't seem to care either. About the time I realized that I didn't care whose ass I was humping on, I also realized that I might be a little too intoxicated for my own good. "Peaches, I'm going back to the room to lie down."

"OK, I'm coming with you." She didn't seem intoxicated at all.

"You don't have to come with me, Peaches. I'm good."

## Don't Ask, Don't Tell

"Oh, I'm not staying, D. I'm just making sure you're OK. I'm going back to the party. Tonight is my sober night and I already picked out who I am going to *ride, baby babay!* I'm setting it up, now. You won't see me again until the morning."

"Do you, P," I told her as I focused on putting one foot in front of the other.

We walked down the hall to our door. Right before we got there, guess who turned the corner? Sealyn, beautiful Sealyn and I was drunk again. "Dahni, isn't that your friend?" Peaches got Sealyn's attention. "Hey. What's up? I've seen you before. I'm Peaches. Me and Dahni go to the same church at home."

"Hi, I'm Sealyn. It's nice to meet you." Sealyn smiled.

"Hi Sealyn," I said. Sealyn stopped smiling. She could tell I was lit.

"What up, D?" she said kind of flip like.

"Well, Dahni are you good? Open the door and go in the room." Peaches was ensuring my safety.

"Sealyn, this chick is drunk. Do you mind going inside to talk with her if y'all are going to talk? I want to make sure she is inside before I go and take care of some things tonight!"

Sealyn laughed. "Peaches, you are a trip girl."

"Sealyn, you don't have to come in if you don't want to. See you, Peaches, " I said.

Sealyn turned to me. "Dahni, I'm a grown ass woman. I know what I have to do and don't have to do." She walked around me and went inside the room. She seemed like she was rushing inside the room.

I walked in and fell face first on the bed. "Dahni, what have you been drinking and why?" I stayed in my stretched out position.

"I'm partying, Sealyn. Can I do that? I only had a few shots. I ate. I danced most of it off. I have a nice buzz. I'm cool. Mind your business. What have you been up to?"

"Nigga, is that all you have to say after you just fucking ignored me for more than a month? What have I been up to, Dahni? You asshole, asswipe, ass! What the hell do you mean what have I been up to? Damn, you make me sick!"

I sat up. "All that from one question?" I smiled.

"Dahni, I'm not playing with you. This is not funny to me."

"OK, OK." She blew my high.

"But seriously, Sealyn. What have you been doing?"

"I've been licking my freaking wounds. After you ignored me on the bus, did not respond to my letter that I put directly in your hands, and after you ignored the messages I left for you at the duty desk, I've just been licking my damn wounds!"

"Messages? You didn't leave any messages for me, Sealyn."

"You's a lie! Now you want to lie, Dahni? I left you five messages with my information. That's why I cussed your ass out in the club. Now tonight because you have a buzz, you want to talk? Talk about what? We don't have anything to talk about!" Sealyn got up and started walking toward the door. In my mind I was thinking, "What the hell did you come in the room for then?" But I didn't say it.

I jumped up and grabbed her. "I didn't get any messages from you, Sealyn. Not one."

"Liar. Get off me! You're drunk now. That's the only time you're brave enough to face who you really are ANYWAY! Just leave me alone, Dahni. You are just as fucked up as everybody else and I don't have time for more drama! I have enough in my life as it is." Then Miss Sealyn opened the door and walked out.

Well, damn. I really hadn't received any messages from her. And what did she mean about she had enough drama? That chick was really tripping. Why was she acting like this was a real relationship type situation anyway? The stuff that happened between us couldn't be taken seriously. I didn't mean to hurt her feelings but I wasn't like that. I wasn't a lesbian. What happened with us was just a thing. Regardless, I still feel fucked up right about now. . .

## Dahni McPhail

\*

I woke up the next morning still feeling like shit. It wasn't because of a hangover but because something was tugging at my heart. Sealyn hated me, I thought. I looked over at the other bed and Peaches was in it. I guess she didn't get what she wanted last night.

I walked outside on the balcony watched the sunny morning goings on. I stood there looking around trying to figure out where to get something to eat. I saw a fast food restaurant across the street and decided to go and get some food and coffee. I made a mental note to bring back something for Peaches. I knew she'd be hungry when she got up.

As I walked down the hall, I passed a room where some females were screaming their heads off. I thought, *damn. What are they doing arguing this early in the morning?* I figured they must have never gone to sleep and were still drunk.

"Bitch, I will kick your fucking ass if I find out you are fucking around on me!"

Hmmm... That type of argument, huh? Dykes were everywhere. Those voices sounded familiar.

I went to the restaurant. I guess the people working there weren't feeling their jobs because they took extra damn long to get the few things I ordered. I felt like I was in there for an hour. Damn! I gratefully took the food from the cashier's hands and started out the door toward the hotel.

That's when I saw the Black Audi spin out of the hotel driveway and into the street. There was no mistaking that car. It was The Jackal's ride. What was that demon doing down here? All I could think was that some type of trouble followed me here to school and her hateful ass was here to deliver it to me personally. But that was stupid. How could she know I was on pass and in this particular hotel? That wasn't her. It had to be a car that looked like hers.

"Dahni, thank you. Thank you, thank you, thank you, girl. I am starvin like Marvin. What did you get me?" I knew Peaches was going to be hungry.

"Food. I thought you were staying out to get you some dick, chick."

"Girl, one of the Negros that I thought was cute enough to fuck was trying to get with the cute Latino dude who was my second choice to try to fuck. Dick got my dick. Everybody in there was a faggot or a dyke almost," Peaches went on and on and on. It rather offended me to hear her say "dyke" like that. She kept talking. "I thought about letting a chick eat me out to see what its like but I don't want to be disappointed. I like dick too much, girl. Give me some pole to rock up in my hole any day. I'm strictly dickly!" On and on… "But I ain't got nothing against nobody. Do you." she stated. "People might say I'm a ho because I get mine and I don't care. I just ain't about to fuck with no bitches." She stopped to take a breath.

"Well, Peaches. Tonight is another night. There will be several parties and several chances for you to ride Mandingo or latingo or whitedingo."

"Oooh Dahni girl, I hope I can find me a big ole Mandingo dick. Mmmm." I had to look at Peaches and laugh.

"Girl you are crazy."

The parties didn't wait for the sun to go down. They started as soon as people woke up and got dressed. I was down for that. I started going from room to room again to see what was happening. I didn't drink though. I scheduled my buzz time for tonight when all the other chicks are lit. Then I would grind some ass. *OK, now I'm thinking the shit in my sober mind. Help me.*

Many people were out at the pool swimming, chilling and getting drunk at the tiki bar. The scene was nice. There was an Olympic sized pool with lounge chairs around the side. The bar was on a deck with bamboo stools and another dance area. I decided to go out there and chill. That's when I saw Sealyn sitting across the pool with some girl. Sealyn didn't see me. I came up behind her and touched her on the shoulder.

"Scott." She had on sunglasses.

"Hey, McPhail" She said in a sort of "whaddaya want" kind of way. "Gina, this is McPhail. McPhail, this is my friend Gina."

## Don't Ask, Don't Tell

"Hi, Gina." Gina looked me up and down. I was wearing a wife beater and some long cargo shorts.

"Damn, Sealyn." Gina looked at Sealyn in a knowing way. What was up with that?

"What are you doing today Sealyn? Let's go and hang out a little bit. Or just walk down to the beach with me right now. I'm sober." Sealyn smiled at me.

"No, that's OK. I'm going up to my room to chill after I finish chilling out here."

"Well, can you just come here for a minute then, Sealyn? Please?" She sighed and got up to walk with me.

"What do you want, Dahni?"

"Sealyn, I just want to tell you that I really did not get any messages from you. You know I'm not rude enough to ignore someone who is trying to get in touch with me—"

"Yes you are rude enough," she cut me off. "Especially if you don't want to be bothered. Why don't you just say the rest of what you really need to say, Dahni. You want to forget about everything that happened!"

"Um, could you stop being so loud, please?" I asked, darting my eyes around to see who was nearby.

"Stop talking to me then, Dahni, dammit, if you're worried about people hearing your conversation." She was pissed off again. "Come on, Gina. Can we go, please?" Sealyn picked up her stuff and started walking down toward the beach. So, I followed her. "Why are you following me, Dahni? Leave me alone."

"I'm not following you. I'm just walking in the same direction that you are." She quickly made a hard right.

"See, you're following us. This is harassment." She finally went to some chairs under an umbrella and sat down with Gina. Gina laughed the whole way.

I smiled a slick little smile at Sealyn's friend. "So you're laughing at me, Gina. Am I funny?" I asked her.

"Yeah, Dahni. You are funny." Gina said that in a weird and knowing way. Then both she *and* Sealyn laughed at her remark. I didn't get it. "Dahni, do you like Sealyn?" Gina asked me. What the fuck was this girl trying to prove asking me that shit?

"Yeah. Sealyn is cool with me."

"No, I mean do you *like* Sealyn. Like as in boy/ girl, but its girl/ girl type action. Do you like my friend?" I looked at Gina's pretty but smart mouthed self, got up, and walked away thinking, *Freakin' crab.*

Sealyn screamed behind me, "See, that's why I'm not even trying to deal with you, Dahni McPhail. That's exactly why!"

## Don't Ask, Don't Tell

I started running and I didn't stop until I got to my room. Oh my Gosh! Did Sealyn tell that girl about us? How could she do that? Why would Gina ask me some shit like that if she didn't know what happened? Fucking Sealyn. She's going to ruin my rep. I know if Peaches hears that shit Peaches will tell everyone at home about it and my parents will curl up and die. That fuckin' dyke. I had to get control of that shit.

\*

As we got ready for the nighttime parties, Peaches and I went over our plan for the evening's activities. Peaches' plan was plain and simple. Find a cute permanent party guy and get some dick. My plan was to party a lot, drink a little and put some stuff to the back of my mind.

That's what I did and that's what Peaches did. We had a blast. Now the pool party was in full swing. A DJ was on the scene and she was awesome. We were dancing and kicking it. We were there for an hour when Peaches walked by me with her victim for the night. She winked at me. That let me know her "pole" was secure for the evening and I would be alone in my room.

It was get fucked up time now. I drank a couple of shots and kept dancing around through the crowds of intoxicated women and men doing my usual booty hump thing. It was one o'clock when I decided to call it quits. We had to get back to the dorms before noon and I wanted to sleep in again. I headed to my room and as I reached my door, I saw Sealyn leaving a note underneath it. Was she fucking crazy? Did she not know that I had a roommate? I had to get this chick straight right now!

Sealyn started walking away. I ran up on her and grabbed her. I pushed her against my door. "Look you're going to have to stop fucking putting my business in the street! Do you understand me?" I was drunk. I didn't think I still was, but I was. I grabbed her by the shoulders and shook her. "Do you?" I squeezed her arms hard--too hard.

Then the woman scared the shit out of me. Sealyn sank to the floor and started pleading. She dropped everything in her hands and cowered on the floor. "Please don't hit me. Please, Dahni." She was bawling. I was completely shocked by her reaction. What the. . .? "Please Dahni, I'm sorry." Instinctively, I reached down, grabbed her up, and held her in my arms. What in the hell was going on with this chick?

"What's wrong with you? Why are you acting like that? I'm not going to hit you, Sealyn. Come on." I opened my door and took her inside. I sat her on the edge of the bed. "I'm sorry. I'm not--I mean I would never put my hands on you. Well, I would never hurt you or punch you--hit you." She was still crying. "Sealyn, look at me." She looked at me and what I saw ignited rage in my heart. She had a swollen, bruised eye. I looked at her pretty face with all the tears and the swelling. "Sealyn, what happened to you? Who hit you?" She covered her face.

"Dahni, just forget about it. You can't help me. This is my problem."

## Don't Ask, Don't Tell

"Is it your ex? Is it your ex because I will break that motherfucker off tonight! The bitch needs somebody who can go toe to toe!" I was seething.

"Dahni, please." Sealyn started crying again making me even madder. My heart broke watching her. It was like she was crying for more than me shaking her at my door.

"I need to go. I need to leave, Dahni." She got up.

"I can't let you leave while you're like this, Boo." *Boo?* "I ain't like that other motherfucker." I went into the bathroom, got a warm washcloth for her face and wiped her tears. She started to calm down.

"Dahni, I was just leaving you a letter to let you know that I have not shared our information with anyone. I would never do that. I also was letting you know that I graduate before you and I'm going to my first permanent party duty station. My school is not as long as yours. And that I love you, I forgive you and I don't hold anything against you." Graduating *and* leaving? Damn. I just found her again. "And Dahni. . ."

I didn't give her a chance to tell me whatever she was going to say. I grabbed her face and kissed her. *Leaving?* I kissed her with everything that I had. "You're leaving? You can't leave me." I pushed her back on the bed and continued to kiss her as if it was the last kiss ever. I didn't have many skills, but I remembered everything she had done to me. I also knew what I wanted to do to her. I kissed her deeply, repeatedly. I took a minute to commit her beauty to memory. Sealyn's mother was

## Dahni McPhail

Native American and her father was African American. Her caramel color was enhanced by soft black hair, black eyebrows and long, thick eyelashes. Thick, kissable lips complimented her tender features. Her teeth were naturally straight and beautiful. She smiled at me. I took off her shirt and she looked at me intently. I kissed her again. With more ambition than skills, I began making love to every part of her body with my mouth. Her neck, her breasts, her belly. I felt like I had to absorb her. I tasted her nipples and gently bit them. Simultaneously, I ran my hands all over her body. I kissed her in the same places she kissed me and she reacted the way I did. She moved her body toward my lips.

I licked her navel and kissed her stomach. I massaged her thighs and every crevice with my mouth. Now, I'm not even going to lie. I was scared as fuck to put my mouth on her pussy. But I had to. I just really wanted to taste her and be inside her that night. I parted her tenderly and took her clit into my mouth, tasting her juices. She was salty/sweet. It was actually good. I never thought I could enjoy doing this to a woman, but I was feeling the situation. I made love to her as best as I knew how. I slid my tongue inside every fold. Deep inside her. That felt good to my tongue. It was so warm and wet inside her that I kept sliding my tongue in and out. Somewhere in the distance, she was moaning and calling my name. I kept loving her with my tongue while she writhed against my mouth. Her wetness was all over my face. After a few more strokes I felt her tremble. Sealyn grabbed my arms, scratching my biceps. I just let her hold on for the ride. That night was the first time I made love to a woman.

# Don't Ask, Don't Tell

## Chapter 8

I don't know how to explain it but there was some type of emotional thing in my heart for Sealyn. After I finished making love to her, she lay in my arms. I held her close to me. I really wanted her to know that I cared for her and that I didn't want her to be hurt. That I would try to be there as much as I could. I didn't say these words to her. I didn't say anything. I just kissed her face until I fell asleep.

"Get up, Dahni!" I felt a hard smack on my ass.

"Damn, Peaches. What the hell is wrong with you?"

"Get up. We need to start getting ready to go, that's what's wrong with me, lazy." Memories of last night flooded my mind. Peaches was standing there while Sealyn might still be in the room. Oh, shit! I was officially fucked in the non-sexual sense. I looked around the room wildly. It seemed like Sealyn was gone.

"Dahni, get your crazy ass up. Why are you acting so weird? Stop drinking that fucking Patron and you won't feel like you have mad cow disease the next day!" Peaches had no idea what I was thinking about, what I was freaking out about inside. I got up and went to the bathroom. On my way there I inspected everything. Neither Sealyn nor her things were still in the room. Not a trace. Nothing except a letter I spotted on my jeans that I left on the floor.

"Did you get the dick last night, P?" Trying to make conversation.

"Did I get it? Did I get it? Hell yeah. Dude was capable, do you hear me?"

"Alright now."

"Ate my pussy too. That's why I'm not fucking with him anymore. If we had just fucked, that would have been all right. But you don't eat nobody's pussy that fast. If he did it to me, he'll do it to someone else." Life lessons. "Well, I might fuck with him again. I'm just never going to kiss him."

OK, no questions yet. That meant Peaches did not run into Sealyn on the way out or even know that Sealyn was in here last night. Yes! I'm safe. I couldn't have anybody thinking that I'm a dyke. I just had some temporary sympathy for Scott but I'm not a homo. I picked up the letter off my pants and went to take a shower.

"I saw your friend leave, Dahni." I froze in my tracks. Terror ripped through my heart and I began explaining.

"Oh she was drunk and I just wanted to help her out."

"What are you talking about, fool? I saw her leaving the hotel this morning on my way back here. She got in this nice ass car with some chick and pulled off."

"Oh, she left?" The terror of being discovered turned into the disappointment of Sealyn leaving without saying anything to me. I guess she was just paying me back, though.

"It must have been somebody she knew. She hugged the chick and got in the car. She had bags with her, so I guess she had checked out and all."

I barely heard Peaches' words as I went into the bathroom madder than a muthafugga. "That fucking lesbian, freaky ass bitch," I thought. Sealyn just wanted me to do that nasty shit to her! She played me and then left with who the fuck ever Peaches saw her with! Damn her! "Girl, let me get in the shower," I croaked out a few words to Peaches. "I'm sure we'll run into each other again."

"Hurry up, D, because I need a shower too and I want to lie down again for 30 minutes before we go back to deal with the bullshit."

## Don't Ask, Don't Tell

I closed the bathroom door. I turned on the shower as hot as I could stand it and got in. The water hit my face and I started to cry. I mean really cry. I had this aching pain in my chest. It felt like I could reach inside my body, grab the pain and pull it out. The tears flowing from my eyes were so hot they felt like they were burning my face. I sat down on the side of the tub, put my head in my hands and just fucking sobbed. I could not describe what was happening to me. All I knew was that I could not control my tears. My body shook as I thought about what that fucking bitch had done to me. What she had turned me into. Then to just leave after I. . . "Dahni, hurry the hell up!" I tried to regain my composure.

"OK. OK, Peaches, dang. I'm almost ready."

It took everything in me to get my shit together so I could face other humans. I stepped out of the shower and dried off, put on my boxers and walked out into the room. "With your slow ass. You act like no one else has to use the bathroom." Peaches just didn't know. I had to shoot a comment back so she wouldn't notice my mood. "Old lady, shut the hell up." I said. "I mean, dirty old lady. You're that lady on Barclay Street in the old rickety house. The one everyone was scared of who molested the young boys."

Peaches laughed. "Even an old ho needs some pole every now and again."

Peaches went into the bathroom. I got dressed and gathered my things. That's when I saw the letter Sealyn left on my toiletry bag.

"Bitch!" I tore up the letter and put it in the side pocket of my gym bag to make sure no one else would find it. I hated Sealyn.

\*

The rest of school training went by in a blur. We spent our time working like hell to keep our averages as high as possible. On the weekends, we partied. I was drinking and getting in my free feels as much as I could and still not acknowledging my behavior. Peaches kept sleeping with Mandingo coochie eater every weekend. I didn't want to deal with anyone. Relationships and feelings were the absolute last thing on my mind.

"I never thought I'd say this, but I'll be so glad to get back to school, Dahni. I don't know what I'm going to do."

"I don't have school ahead of me, but I'll be gone from here soon and going to my first duty station. At least I'll be out of the training environment. No more drill sergeants, classes, and other crap. Know what I mean, Peaches? They say it's just like having regular a job."

"Yeah, Dahni. I'm sure it'll be nice"

Graduation came and went without a hitch. The two partying-est people in the class got the highest averages and scored the highest in all their additional military training. Dahni and Peaches. Neither of us thought we were at the top of the class. We really didn't care. Our goal was a weekly goal. We did everything we did to ensure we could leave on Fridays and not have to come back until Sunday. Oh well, whatever the reason. We kicked ass. Now it was time to get on our planes and get on with the rest of our lives.

"Dahni, girl, it was awesome being here in school with you. I couldn't ask for a better partna. You're my sister. I'm going to miss you." Sexy Peaches hugged me.

"I'm gonna miss you too. The best thing about us, Peaches, is that we're truly home girls. So, we're never going to lose touch with each other."

"I know that's right. Are you gonna be home for the holidays, D?"

"You know it, Peaches. I'll be over your parent's house to eat."

"Yeah. We're gonna have to figure out a way to ditch the family, though." Ditch the family. I'd forgotten about the fact that we aren't adults back at home.

"That should be easy now. They know we're here together. When we get home, we'll be able to do what we want to do--for the most part-- as long as we make it to church on Sundays."

"Yeah. That's gonna be strange as hell having to ask can we go somewhere. Oh well. We can play the game. That way we know we'll be able to get it all in."

We talked and laughed until it was time to board our planes. Peaches was going back to Temple and I was headed to Germany. Yeah, Germany. I was excited. I wanted the experience. What I really wanted was "away." Far, far, away.

I arrived in the Federal Republic of Germany not knowing a single soul. I was scared shitless. This was when I really started loving the military because once I was assigned to my unit, they sent a sponsor to come and pick me up. They took me to the billeting office and I signed for the key to my room. They briefed me and dropped me off at my dorm, and I was free to do as I wanted until it was time to report to work. My sergeants made sure I had someone to take me around and train me on what I needed to know about the job and about the area. Best of all, the workday was from six a.m. to five p.m. and then we were off work like regular human beings. Besides training to fight wars, it was just a regular job and it was all right with me.

I learned the ropes quickly and figured out that I only had to do a couple of things to make my life easy. Those things were: be where I'm supposed to be and do what I'm told. Too easy! I assimilated, kept my nose clean and followed the rules.

Being the new girl on the block made me special around the unit. I was the latest piece of ass that the guys were trying to get. I had to laugh so I wouldn't be completely disgusted. There were so many dudes doing nice things for me. They all thought that because I just turned 19, I was stupid. They were unaware that I had six older brothers who were handsome devils--level ten womanizers--who taught me well and briefed me constantly before I departed their personal training facility. Besides that, I was used to guys and their stupid shit everywhere I went. Dahni wasn't giving up any ass. But Dahni would spend your money, mister.

After a few months, the guys figured out that they were not getting any sex from me and they moved on to the next group of new chicks. I tried to warn the ones that I could but most of the new girls never had this much attention in their lives, nor were they privy to my scholarly brothers. So, they usually ended up being passed around, talked about or pregnant within a short time. The fathers of their children were usually married--but never mentioned it--and vehemently denied responsibility. It was a vicious circle.

That's why when my new roommate arrived I took her under my wing. Some of it may have been because she was Korean and Black and fine, fine, beautiful, fine. *There you go again, Dahni.* Flawless russet skin, hazel eyes, sculptured and full lips. Not that I was looking at her. I was past that shit. There was nothing wrong with giving another woman her props. I am not now, nor had I ever been a hater. The rest of why I took her under my wing was because she was really naïve--or so I thought. Her dad was a military officer and her mama was from a holy sanctified church where she wasn't even allowed to wear pants. She left college and snuck into the military. She came in the door trying to escape from family drama. Well, she was my roommate now. I, at least, would keep an eye on her and make sure she was OK.

"Mianya. Mee-an-ya, that's how you say my name."

"OK, hi. I'm Dahni. Dah-Nee. That's how you say mine." We walked down the hallway to our room. I pointed openly at a guy walking past us. "See that bastard right there? Take his money and don't give him any. He's married and has three kids. His wife is in the states."

Mianya looked surprised. "Dahni, you're crazy girl! How do you know all this?"

"They all tried to get some from me when I first got here. You can do what you want but I'm just trying to tell you. If you end up pregnant, everyone is going to scatter to the winds and you'll be like her." I pointed at Daniels. "A pregnant private, soon to be a single parent, with no father stepping up to the plate. Ya don't want that."

I turned the key, opened our room door and walked in with Mianya following me. When they told me I was getting a roommate, I pushed the wall lockers in the middle, separating the room. I gave her the side by the window with the most privacy. I set up a common area in the front where we both had room to plug in our computers or other electronic gear. We had one bathroom inside the room. It was decent.

## Don't Ask, Don't Tell

I sat down at my desk and got on my laptop. She walked over and sat on her bed. "I don't even like guys, McPhail." *Screeeeeeeeeeeeeeeeech!* I stopped in my tracks. I turned toward her.

"What did you say?" All of a sudden, I was nervous as hell. Did she just say that she was a dyke? I know I am not about to have to deal with that bullshit again. And in my room with me every freaking day?

"I said I don't even like guys. I just keep to myself. I'm not looking for a relationship or a husband. I just want to be free to breathe. I want to be away from my parents, church, college and everything! I just want to be free!"

Whew! That girl scared the shit out of me for a minute! "I feel you. I'm not interested in anyone either. I hang out with a couple of friends. I work. Go to the games and on the company trips. Site see. School. But that's about it. I love everybody but I don't deal with many people. Especially females. It's less drama. And please don't feel any kind of way if I don't hang with you all day every day. It has nothing to do with you. But I'll be here for you if you are cool with me."

"Ok, I'm with you on that. I think we will understand each other very well, Dahni. You're pretty mature for your age."

"Thanks, I don't know why I hear that a lot. For real because in the next five minutes I'm going to do some stupid shit. Watch." We both laughed. She was laughing at me and I was laughing a laugh of relief. She's straight.

## Dahni McPhail

To be 24 years old, Mianya hadn't been around much but she was making up for lost time. That chick was in the wind every weekend. Nothing bad. She was just touring Europe every chance she got. She knew one chick from somewhere and then made some other friends. I still hung out with my boys Adrian and Krys. We'd bought some equipment and started our own little DJing business. Mianya and her friends always came to our gigs. They were nice chicks. I could see they cared a lot about her. They seemed tight, but for some reason, Mianya always brought her questions, problems and issues to me. I guess it was because we lived together.

"Dahni, can I ask you something?"

"Is it personal? Because you know I don't answer personal questions before nine p.m."

She laughed. "Yeah, it's personal but please make an exception today."

"OK, what's up?"

"Why don't you date anybody? I mean you are really hot." *Did she say hot?* "You've got mad DJ skills. You are outstanding at your job. Why do you just hang out with those two goofy guys instead of dealing with someone up close?"

"I thought you were going to ask me something for yourself."

## Don't Ask, Don't Tell

"This is for me, Dahni. You're my friend. We've been roommates for months and you just work, and play your music. You don't interact with anyone on an intimate level."

"Mianya, I don't want to fuck around with emotions."

"Well, who says you have to get emotional? You can just socialize more than you do." I stood there and looked at Mianya. What was wrong with the girl today?

"Mimi, I like what I do. I have a lot of fun. I go places and see things and make a lot of extra money that I spend on my bad habits."

"What did you call me?" Mianya looked at me strangely. "Oh. Mimi. I thought it up. You're special to me now."

"Thanks, Dahni, and back to the subject. You don't have anyone special in *your* life, Dahni."

"Neither do you, Mimi." Mimi put her hands on her hips and cocked her head.

"How do you know if I don't have anyone special in my life? Stop and think about it. You don't even know, do you? No. You don't. Why? Because you won't even allow yourself to get emotionally invested in our friendship." What a look she gave me.

"Did you take psychology or something in college?" I tried to be flip.

## Dahni McPhail

"And every time, Dahni, I try to talk to you seriously about getting involved with people you make a joke out of it. Everything is not a joke, McPhail"

I heard those words before. I had to end this chatter right now. "Mianya, what do you want me to do? How is it that I might invest my emotions in our friendship? You want me to cry? You act like I don't care about you at all. If anybody fucks with you, they have me to deal with. I care. I just don't be all up in your grill."

"You don't have to be *up in my grill.* I just want you to be a better friend. A closer friend. Yes, I can trust you and I know I don't have to worry about anyone stepping to me. I know I can confide in you but you never, ever go anywhere nor do anything with me. You just hang out with ya boys." *Yeah, because they don't do all this damn talking and reading of the minds.*

"So, Mimi. You're taking me through all this conversation so I can hang out with you and your giggling ass friends? You want me to come to your tea parties?" I turned back to my laptop.

"Tea parties? Shiiiddd... You better ask. I think I just told you that I want you to hang out with me. It won't be at a tea party, though. I want to hang out with you outside this room--with other humans--occasionally. Is that too much to ask?" *Yes*

## Don't Ask, Don't Tell

"Naw. It's not too much to ask. What do you want me to do?" Why did I ask that question? When Friday hit, we got off work early and hit the streets.

"Bring enough clothes to wear and to go out all weekend. Can you bring your DJ gear and your Ipod?"

"Mimi, why the fuck do we need that? See, I knew I shouldn't be—"

"Shush it! Stop the whining and just bring the shit, McPhail!"

Well all right holy sanctified daughter of a Colonel. Somebody, obviously, is out they mama house! I got everything and put it in my bag. Mimi's friend Trish came and picked us up in her car. She had her own apartment so we went over there first. We dropped off our stuff and then we went everywhere! I mean, I thought me and my boys went everywhere but this was a different kind of everywhere, a nicer everywhere. On the way back to Trish's apartment, Mimi asked her "do you have what Dahni needs to hook up for the party?" *Party?*

"What party?"

"Dahni, Trish is having a party at her place tonight. I volunteered you to DJ."

"And I'm getting ready to volunteer to whoop your ass too. Mimi, why didn't you tell me? I would have done it for you regardless. But you could have told me."

"I'm asking you now." *Smart-ass.*

"We've just invited a few friends over to kick it and have some drinks. It should be fun." We, huh? I knew I should have gone with my boys.

I quickly realized that--as she said--I didn't know the woman I share a room with at all. A few fucking friends actually meant a boatload of nothing but women. There had to be about fifty or more women in this two-story townhouse and more out in the back on the lawn. And guess who still hadn't figured out yet that they all were lesbians. Yes, me. Dahni McPhail. I used to be so lost.

"Mimi, you're a lying ass chameleon ass sneaky female, and I wanted to compliment you face-to-face on that. But since I'm here, where do you want me to set up?" What I said must have amused her because she laughed.

"The table is right over here."

"What do you want me to play and how long do you want me to play?"

"Just put on something for now. You won't really have to play until everyone gets here later."

"So, this isn't everyone Mimi?"

"Not by a long shot. Don't worry Dahni. I got you"

## Don't Ask, Don't Tell

The last time I heard *those* words I ended up crying my eyes out in a hotel bathroom. Well, this definitely wasn't that. I put on my first mixed song list so something could be playing while everyone walked around and mingled.

*

The party was turning out to be nice. I didn't know there were that many women in Germany. Definitely not in one city. I'd never seen them anyway. I figured this was some type of group, fraternity, or organization party because it was getting dark and there still were no guys there. I mean, there were a few gay guys. Regardless of the attendees, I tell you what. Those women knew how to party. They had mega shit. Plenty of food. I ate about three times. Lots to drink. I was gonna have my first shot in a few minutes. It was all just nice.

Mianya came over to me being extra friendly. "Mimi, you been drinkin'?" I asked the obvious. She moved close to me and slid her arm up massaging the back of my head with her hand. I was wearing my hair down like Snoop. A voice in my head said, *"This is one pretty woman. Damn."* I didn't chastise myself for that thought. Any woman or man would have thought the same. But the hand thing. . . "Mimi?"

"You know, Dahni, you're the one who gave me that nickname. You were the first person to call me that. Now everybody calls me Mimi." She was smiling and drunk.

## Dahni McPhail

"Girl, I didn't feel like calling you that crazy shit your parents named you. What you been drinking? Why didn't you bring me something?"

"I didn't know you wanted anything."

"Yeah, hook me up, Mimi. Bring me a shot of Patron and a beer." I had to get her hands off me.

I was building a tolerance for alcohol. It was essential to my survival. All I hung around with were military guys and there was a requirement for me to be able to manage my shit. My friends I could trust, but not those other dudes. They were always telling me I was pretty. Adrian and Krys didn't care what I looked like as long as I could mix songs while they went and picked up DJ Groupies for the night.

Mimi brought back my drinks. I took the shot and followed it with a beer. "You want another shot?"

"Yeah, just gimme one more. I don't wanna be fucked up trying to DJ and play some dumb shit by mistake." Mimi stood there and looked at me for a minute. Then she smiled and went to get another shot for me. *What was that about?*

"You want anything. . .else?" Ever so coyly, Mimi asked the question.

"Mi,"—now I had broken her name down to one syllable—"You're drunk, ain't you?"

## Don't Ask, Don't Tell

"No, I just have a nice buzz. Thanks for coming to play for us tonight." She reached up and gave me a hug. Then kissed me on the cheek. Then hugged me some more. I stepped back.

"Are you gonna thank me for an hour, girl? Take your ass somewhere and let me play this music." Mimi laughed and told me to let her know if I wanted anything else as she walked away.

No. I didn't want anything just then. It was time to get it crunk in that muthafugga there! I started spinning the latest tunes. At first, there wasn't anyone in the dancing room, but when they heard me in there mixing it up, they all came in to watch. A couple of the women came up to me and asked me if I have any business cards. I was prepared. I pulled out my cards and gave them one. One chick wrote her number on the back and handed it to me. Mimi walked up and looked at the women like she was going to scratch their eyes out. Why was my roommate crazy tonight? I drank another shot and continued cranking the music.

Everybody was on the floor dancing after a while. I still didn't notice anything until I played a semi-slow song so I could run to the bathroom. I ran to the upstairs bathroom because it was off limits and I knew there would be no wait. When I came back downstairs to continue playing, the damn Lesbos were all in there slow dancing with each other! Mianya hauled ass over to where I stood. She must have been watching and waiting for me to come down the steps. I could tell by the look on her face that I had a look on mine.

"Dahni, you OK? You're not going to trip in here, are you?" I was still standing there watching girls with girls all wrapped up kissing and grinding and dancing to the slow song I played. Then I turned and looked at Mianya.

"You set me up and that was fucked up, Mianya. All these chicks you hang out with are dy—lesbians?"

"Yeah, Dahni. Everybody here is "family." That's what we call it."

"What do you mean, 'We' Mimi? You too?" Dammit, dammit, damn! Here we go with this shit again!

"Yeah. Me too. So you're not my friend anymore?"

"Nah you know I ain't even like that, we cool. But you didn't have to fuckin' lie and set me the hell up. That was the fucked up part. If I were a different type of person, I would knock your ass out right now. But I'm not the type to just jump on people, and I'm not like *that* either," I said looking toward the lesbians. "I'm ready to go."

"Dahni, don't leave. I'm sorry, Dahni. Please forgive me. I really am sorry." She was getting upset. "Please just finish playing for the party and don't curse anybody out and I will make sure you get back to the room tonight. I promise." Mimi looked at me and a tear rolled down her cheek. For some reason, a woman crying just does something to me.

"Mimi, I said I wasn't mad at you." *Stop the fuggin' crying.* I walked up to her and hugged her. "How could I be mad at my room dawg? I just didn't know what was up. You should have told me. OK? Will you get me another shot and a beer, please? So I can get fucked up and forget where I am."

"OK. Dahni, I'm sorry. Are you uncomfortable?"

"No. Actually I'm having fun." *But now I'm nervous as hell since my dumb ass--after being here for hours--just realized I'm in a den of dykes.* "I'm cool." Mimi slid her arms up around my neck, pulled me to her and hugged me—her fingers rubbing the back of my head. She needed to stop doing that thing.

The song ended so I had to get back over there to my equipment and get the party crunk again. I had to stop all this slow dancing shit before I had a nervous break down. Mianya brought my drinks over to me with some food and sat them down. Then she gave me another hug and said, "Thanks, Dahni." Then she gave me a big kiss on my cheek. The tipsy woman's friendly kiss caused a tingling in my loins.

Dahni McPhail

## Chapter 9

With my newfound information, I saw the whole party in a brand new light. There were so many chicks I knew from around post, a lot of the ball players and female leaders. All of them were in here huddled up with their girlfriends. Ain't that some shit? You just never know. Well, to each his/her/its own. As long as they are happy and they aren't trying to get with me. My one experience for life was over. There would be no more.

I continued drinking and felt myself getting tipsy so I had to dance it off. People say that I can dance but I don't think so. I just get into it when I'm DJing and I start doing my thing behind the DJ stand all by myself. That's what I was doing when Mimi came up to me and said, "Oh my goodness. I live with you and I ain't know you could work it like that! You don't have to stay behind there and play all night. Nobody's gonna bite you, Dahni. Come dance."

"No."

"Dance with me." I motioned for Mimi to come closer and started smiling before she got close.

"Fuck no. You're gonna touch my ass!" She knew I was messing with her. She grabbed my hand and made me come out on the dance floor with her. Now, all other times I was drinking and humping on butts or dancing with anyone really didn't count. This was my first time dancing with a girl for real, for real. I didn't know how I was supposed to dance.

"Don't get mad, Dahni." Oh shit, what was she about to say? "You are really pretty, OK? But in these circles, the way you look with your hair down and your athletic build makes you a stud. A stud is a boy/girl. I'm a girl/girl. I said all that to say that you and I can't be doing the same thing out here on the dance floor. Man it up, please. Dance like the other boy/girls that are here. Look around."

"Do you want me to stay out here on the dance floor with you, chameleon girl, or do you want me to leave your ass out here? I'm not dancing like a boy. What kind of shit is that?" I concluded that my roommate was a damn nut job among other things. What kind of sense was she trying to make? Was there another, parallel world with a completely new set of rules for dykes? I mean, lesbians.

Mianya squinted her eyes at me like she was going to tackle me right there. Suddenly, I thought it was in my best interest to comply. I did what she asked me to do. I looked around. I could see the more dominant looking chicks dancing. They were dancing, not like dudes. But. . .I mean they were still kicking it but they were dancing more *dominantly*? In some cases chicks were just doing whatever. I did see what Mimi was talking about though. A few words stuck in my head from Mimi's "lesbian stud lesson." I wanted to go and look in a mirror to check out this "way" that I looked. I had my hair out, a wife beater on and my jeans sagging with some timbs. I didn't get it. I thought I looked cute. I reminded myself to check it out later. I was out on the floor with this girl and didn't want to get embarrassed.

I decided to do a little jig until I got a feel of how to work with Mimi on the floor. The mix I put on switched to this "drop it like its hot" song and Miss Mimi started working the body. I was shocked. This was not the church mouse that showed up on my room step months ago. She swung her hair, dropped down to the floor, and got up. She started poppin thangs. I knew I was drunk because that shit looked gooooood to me!

But I just kept dancing. A few minutes passed and I figured out how to dance with her. That's when it got good. I felt comfortable because I knew her. We were like a team. It was a lot of fun dancing with such a pretty, sexy ass woman. I'm drunk. No sooner than I thought that, Mimi turned around and backed her ass up to me. She backed up directly on my "area" and started winding her ass. Her body was like a part of my body. We melted together. She was strategically located. Mianya was turning me the fuck on right then and there on the dance floor. My heart was beating like crazy. I reached down and grabbed her waist so she could stay right where she was.

Mimi moved away from me and turned around. She looked at my face and bust out laughing. She came close to me and whispered, "Are you OK?"

I said, "Yeah, why?"

"No reason." She knew she was fucking with my mind and everything else.

She grabbed my hands and put my arms around her waist. Then, she moved closer to me and we started dancing intimately. Like a couple. "Mianya, you're going to have these chicks in here thinking that I fuck around like that."

"Shhh. . .Don't worry about what they think. We're friends."

"OK." She drew me closer to her and started body dancing. Then she turned around and put that ass on me again. This time she was real close. She took my hands and wrapped them around her front. Then she reached up and pulled my head close to her face. She started rubbing my head and moving her body against me in a sexy way. I knew she could feel my heart pounding. My heart was about to jump out of my chest, for real.

Mianya turned around toward me again. This time I pulled her into me and wrapped my arms around her as we swayed to the music. She smelled so good and she was so damn sexy. I was lost in the moment. So lost I didn't even see her giggling ass friends over in the corner cheering us on. No, I didn't see them. All I saw was Mimi. I was into what we were doing together out there. That shit was good.

My equipment must have known I was about to get myself in trouble because the shit cut off right as Mimi moved her head back and put her mouth near mine. The silence woke me up. I quickly said, "Excuse me," and went to fix the problem.

I couldn't find anything wrong with the console so I asked Trish to turn on the light. My lamp wasn't enough. When she turned on the light, I saw that someone had tripped over my extension cord. I re-routed the plug and asked for some tape to stabilize it and keep the cord out of the way. Mianya grabbed my hand and said, "There's some tape in the kitchen."

Mimi pulled me in the kitchen to get the tape. As soon as we got in the kitchen, Mimi turned toward me and threw her arms around my neck. A couple was in the kitchen having a heated discussion. I couldn't pay Mianya any attention because both of the girls looked very familiar. I stared at them intently. Mimi saw me focused on something behind us, turned around and said, "Hey, y'all."

## Don't Ask, Don't Tell

"This is, Dahni." When Mimi said my name, they both turned around. "Dahni, these are my friends Sealyn and T." OK. Now it was time to have a stroke. It was Sealyn. . .And The Jackal.

*

Of all the shit I'd seen so far in Germany and of all the shit I had seen in that apartment that night, I still didn't expect to see that shit right there. My girl Sealyn was at the party with her girlfriend. Drill Sergeant Jones! That bitch was here with the person I hated most on the planet earth! "T" or whatever the fuck Mimi just called her.

"Well I'll be damned. If it ain't my Platoon Guide, McPhail." Well, *I'll* be damned. This bitch still scares the shit out of me. *Man up, Dahni! Man up!* "How are you, soldier?" The Jackal was smiling at me. She reached out her hand to shake mine. I couldn't move for a couple of reasons. One, the grey eyed devil was smiling and trying to shake my hand and two, she was in here with Sealyn. Fucking bitch Sealyn was in here with our GOT DAMN drill sergeant. She was fucking Jones all along. Bitch, bitch, bitch, lying bitch. . .

"Dahni are you going to shake her hand?"

I looked at Mianya like she woke me up from a nightmare. "Uh, hi, drill sergeant."

"Girl, don't call me no damn drill sergeant! I'm 'T' now. I'm off drill sergeant status. I'm stationed here in Germany. So is my wife. You remember Sealyn from training, don't you?" *Wife?* Did The Jackal just call Sealyn her wife?

"Uh yeah. What's up, Scott?" Sealyn just looked at me with those eyes. She knew exactly what the fuck I was thinking and she could see the words "lying bitch" flashing across my eyeballs.

In her own universe, Mianya was all happy because there was someone at the party I knew. If *Mianya* only knew… "Me and Sealyn are stationed over here and live together. You've got to come by the house. We're throwing a barbeque next weekend." With every sentence, The Jackal was stabbing my heart over and over again. She was literally killing me with words. Sealyn's ass was just standing there looking at me.

Mimi went inside the drawer, got the tape and handed it to me. "Guys, the DJ has to go! She has to tape this shit down and get this party jumpin' again. We'll talk to you guys later." Thank you, Mianya, for dragging my yellow, immobile ass out the kitchen by the hand. I could not move on my own.

"What's wrong, Dahni?" Mimi felt something from me and was concerned.

"Nothing, Mimi."

"You look like you've seen a ghost. For real. You have no color in your face." "It's only because that was my drill sergeant. She tried to kill my ass in basic training. She hated me. I wasn't sure whether to hit the bitch or shake her hand when she extended it."

"For real? I can believe that. T's ass is crazy enough to do some mean shit like that. She'll be drunk before the night is over and acting like an idiot. It won't be long. Watch. Hopefully she won't jump on Sealyn in here tonight."

The last words that came out of Mianya's mouth almost made me physically sick. The Jackal *was* the one that Sealyn was talking about. The crazy one. It *was* the Jackal's car down there when we were at Fort Goodwing in training--well, at the hotel. All the shit was coming together now. I remembered Sealyn's story about trying to get away from her crazy lover and her lover following her. One thing was not right with the story, though. Sealyn said that the relationship was over. That shit wasn't over. Lying bitch. My thoughts rambled. I told myself, "I bet you that's why The Jackal was kicking her ass because Sealyn was fucking around all the time. Just like she fucked around with me. That's exactly why the Jackal was fighting on her lying bitch, dyke, lesbian, freaky, ac/dc ass!" Then I started feeling sorry for myself. Why did Sealyn have to drag me into her crazy life and do me like that? I wanted to cry again.

"Mimi, get me another shot and a beer, please?"

"K. I'm going to bring you a sandwich too. You're doing too much drinking and not enough eating. In the meantime, get this party crunk, DJ!!!" Mimi didn't know it but she was a lifesaver that night. A tipsy lifesaver. She turned around and before I could get the music on again, she said. "Bitches! I'm here with the DJ. You are authorized to hate now! Ya hoes!" Everybody in the room fell out laughing, including me. This was a side of Mimi I hadn't seen. It was fun too. This Mimi was funny and lively and was exactly what I needed so I wouldn't crawl into the nearest corner and die.

I got the music going again, the lights went out and the party was on. Oh, I was still feeling that pain in my heart from "lying ass" Sealyn. Even though Mimi didn't really know what was going on, she knew I was feeling some kind of way. She stopped drinking and made sure I was OK and had everything that I needed.

As the night went on, I started having fun again. I was purposely drunk as fuck though. I kept asking for shots. After the last one, Mimi said that was it for me. She was not bringing me anymore shots and warned everyone else not to give me anything else either. Miss Mimi was in charge. In my mind, I had control. Shit, I wasn't too drunk to DJ. I tell you that much.

Every once in a while I looked up to see Sealyn and T dancing or talking. Sealyn would quickly turn her eyes away from me and engage the people around her in conversation. Fuck you too, Sealyn! I didn't mean that. I wanted her to at least acknowledge me and act like she saw me. Something. Anything.

All of a sudden, there was a crash on the other side of the room. What the f. . .? Mianya came over to me and said, "I told you."

"What?"

"T is drunk. She just fell over the chair. Trish and T have been friends for a minute. They're just going to take her ass upstairs and put her in the bed as usual. She'll be alright in the morning and ready to do it all again tomorrow night."

My roommate was well versed in these people's behavior. She knew everyone up and down. That's why I never saw her ass from Friday until Monday morning. She was here with these fools. This definitely was an interesting bunch. Nice too--most of them. I could understand the allure.

Trish and one of the boy girls took T upstairs with Sealyn walking behind them. Then Sealyn came back down to the party by herself. Mianya and I were out on the floor dancing and Mimi was putting that ass on me, yet again. My body was disobeying me—especially my mouth. I wish it would tell this woman to stop torturing me. I should have moved.

"Mimi, can I dance with your friend?" It was Sealyn. "Girl, go ahead. I need to run to the bathroom!"

I reached for her. "No!" I tried to get Mimi not to leave but it was too late. She hurried off to fucking pee.

"What's up, McPhail?"

"Sealyn. Woman, I know of all things tonight you ain't about to try to have a conversation with me. Please don't make me curse you out in front of all these people. I'm so fuckin' mad at you right now I'm likely to break my promise not to hit you!"

"Dahni. Asshole. I was just trying to speak to you. I don't want to talk. I just want to dance. Dance with me."

"No, bitch. Yeah, I just straight up called you a bitch. I don't want to dance." She laughed and then grabbed my hand and pulled me. I didn't want to look like there was a problem with Sealyn and me. Everybody was acting like they weren't looking. But they were looking. I'm sure the nosey lesbians were already wondering how we knew each other well enough to be talking in the first place. "Please?" Sealyn said. She gave me the look that I just couldn't resist.

"OK." And my dumb ass fell for it.

We started dancing and I saw that Miss Scott had some moves too. Besides being the best sex I ever had, she could shake that ass. I'm glad the DJ's music was nice. *Personal pat on the back.* After a minute, I was having a ball with Sealyn out there on the dance floor. I almost forgot that she broke my heart to bits. Almost. The song ended and I had to go back to monitor my music.

"Thanks, Dahni."

"No problem, funny girl."

Sealyn started laughing. "There you go with that shit again." We stood there smiling at each other and Mianya walked up to us. She looked at Sealyn like, "Move ho. Get out my girl's face." Mimi was tripping me out all night long.

"Here, Dahni." Mianya shoved a drink in my hand. "You can have one last shot and a beer. I wasn't sure you could handle yourself. I thought you were gonna start acting stupid but I see you can hang. Take this shot with me." Mianya and I ended up taking two shots. Then we stayed up and partied until the thing was completely over and the last person left the apartment.

"That was a nice party, huh, Miss 'I don't want to hang out with lesbians'." Mianya just had to remind me of my earlier antics. I looked at her. She was looking at me like I was candy. Damn. I guess she was feeling nice again.

"Yeah. It really was nice, smart ass Mianya. I'm lit right now. Let me put my equipment up and take a shower so I can get in the bed. I'm ready to crash."

"Good night everybody." Sealyn was about to go upstairs with her insane ass partner.

Mianya asked, "Sealyn, are you OK? Did you have fun?" Mimi is such a pleasant person.

"Yeah, girl. You know all we have to do is wait until psycho-seven passes out." *Did she just call SFC Jones, psycho-seven?* "Then we can all have a good time."

"I know, right," Mianya agreed. I guess these chicks know each other well enough to say those things. Sealyn looked at me as she was going up the stairs. I looked at her and saw something in her eyes. Was it what I used to see? Naaaaah. She left me more than once without a word. And left for me that crazy motherfucker she is going to lay down with upstairs. I know I didn't see "I want you, Dahni" in those eyes.

"Mimi, where am I sleeping?"

"Where'd you put your bags, Dahni?"

"In the same room as you, sarcastic ass. Damn." Mimi laughed.

"You don't mind sleeping with me, do you?"

"No, girl. You are my room squeeze." I went and took a shower then braided my hair so I wouldn't get tangled in it. She took a shower next. We lay in the bed and Mimi moved close to me. She put her back toward me so I could spoon her, I guess. I wrapped my arm around her and pulled her closer. Then she took my hand into her hand and kissed it. Mimi was so sweet.

"Dahni, tell me what's up with you and Sealyn."

Aw, shit. . .

## Chapter 10

"Why do you think something's up between us?"

"Because you nearly passed out when you saw her in the kitchen. Because you and Sealyn were dancing like you were married and looking like something--whatever it was--had seriously happened between you. Because when I told you how T fights on Sealyn, you looked like you wanted to kill somebody. Because when Sealyn went upstairs, you both held each other's gaze until it was impossible to look at each other anymore. Do I need to go on, Dahni?" *Not really.*

"I don't know what you're talking about."

"Is Sealyn the reason why you're so distant? Why you won't even get remotely involved with anyone?"

I released my hold on Mimi and turned my back toward her. I didn't feel like talking about the bitch who was over in the other room with our fucking drill sergeant. The bitch who knew all along and was the reason why our drill sergeant was trying to kill *only* me. I really didn't want to talk about it. "I don't know what you're talking about Mianya. I'm going to sleep." Mimi climbed on top of me, turned me on my back, and just sat there looking at me.

"Tell me, Dahni." I just lay there looking at that silly, determined, pretty woman.

"Mianya, get off me and take your ass to sleep, please. There is nothing to know. Nothing at all." She leaned forward and laid her body completely on top of mine. She put her face in her hands while her elbows were on either side of my head.

"I don't believe you, Dahni McPhail. I really don't. But I'm not going to stress you about it tonight." Her face was directly over mine. Very close. She sighed and rolled off me onto the bed still facing me. "Good night, Dahni." She moved forward and kissed me on my lips. I looked at her, and then I smiled. I knew she was just concerned about my feelings. She was a good friend.

"Mimi, you're something else." I said. She turned around again and backed up on me. I pulled her closed and spooned her. She grabbed my hand and kissed it again.

\*

"Mimi, are you guys gonna come and eat with us? We made breakfast." It was Trish. She stood over Mimi and I while we were lying in the bed. She startled me because she was standing there, but I didn't feel any panic or terror or a need to hide the fact that I was still holding Mianya. Mimi sleepily said, "Yeah." Then she jumped up and turned around to look at me. "Damn, I wasn't dreaming," she said. "Yeah. We're coming." She pushed her hair out of her face and got out of the bed. I laid there. I didn't want to go downstairs with T and Sealyn. That didn't sound like fun to me. Forget some breakfast.

"Dahni, aren't you gonna come? You should eat something."

"I'm not hungry, Mianya." That was a big ass lie. "There's no need for me to go down there." The truth.

"Are you not hungry or do you just not want to go down there? Which one is it?" Why is every woman a damn investigator?

"Will you go down stairs, Mianya, and stop drilling me this early in the morning? That's which one it is."

"You don't want to go downstairs because of ole girl, huh? Because of Sealyn?" Why is Mimi starting shit early this morning? Why for? Just woke up starting shit.

"That's not it. I just don't know anybody. They probably all think I slept with you and hit that last night and you know I don't get down like that." Mimi completely stopped what she was doing and walked over to my side of the bed.

"Let me tell you something, Negro. They don't think you got with *this* last night, Dahni McPhail, because I'm not sleeping with you or anyone else the first night we hang out together. I don't know what you think you're workin' with but it ain't so good that I'm going to give you some ass the first night. I ain't no ho and my friends know it. So you're wrong. My friends all know *I* don't get down like that. . .With ya conceited ass." She had her hands on her hips. Time to get out of the bed and shut her up.

"Mianya, look at what I'm doing. I'm getting out of the bed." Gee whiz!

We walked down the stairs. One chipper person. One severely apprehensive person dreading what was waiting for me at the breakfast table. "Good morning everybody." Mimi was greeting the masses.

"What's up, y'all." There were about six people downstairs eating. They were chilling at the table. The chicks looked at me and then looked at Mianya.

"Damn, Mimi! How y'all duuuuurrrriinnng!" Everybody at the table fell out laughing. I didn't get the joke. Mianya looked at me and smiled.

"Everybody, this is Dahni."

"Oh, we know who it is girl, but heeeyyy, Dahni."

One of the women said, "Dahni it's so nice to finally meet you. We've heard so much about you."

## Don't Ask, Don't Tell

"About me?" I was puzzled. Mimi looked at the chick like she could choke the life out of her. The woman turned her face in the opposite direction, smiling.

"Well the dead have arisen!" Trish joked. Everybody looked toward the stairs. The Jackal and Sealyn came walking down smiling and fully dressed. "Good morning, everybody. Y'all we can't stay we have to run down town and pick up some. . ."

I wasn't even listening. Everything The Jackal said was "We." Fuckin' "we." Sealyn was right behind that idiot with the "We."

"But we'll be at the crib around two if y'all want to come over. We're watching movies tonight. Everybody at the table—including Mianya's ass—-was like, "Yeah. That sounds like a plan. We ain't doing nothing else but recovering today."

The Jackal turned to me. "McPhail, you coming over to the house?" I almost jumped to my feet and shouted, "Yes, Drill Sergeant!"

I controlled that urge and replied, "I don't know. I have a few things I need to get done today. I'm supposed to be DJing another party tonight." I could feel Mianya's eyes on me because she knew my schedule. She knew I was lying.

"Alright y'all. Well it was nice. We'll see y'all later." Sealyn only said a few words. Was TJ the only one allowed to talk? Sealyn wouldn't even meet my gaze. Mianya was meeting it, though. I looked away from her.

As soon as Sealyn and TJ walked out the door, everybody in the house started talking. "Girl, I don't know why Sealyn stays with T. T just drinks and drinks and acts crazy."

"Yeah, it's a wonder T didn't jump on Sealyn for dancing with Dahni last night."

"That's because she doesn't know and don't nobody tell her either." Trish sent out a serious directive to everyone at the table. "You know how she is." The houseguests who were too drunk to drive last night continued talking.

"Sealyn is too cute to go through that. Sealyn has her degree. She has a lot going for herself. Why does she stay with that idiot?" As they talked and talked, I realized Sealyn was telling the truth about one more thing. She was in a situation that she just couldn't get away from. The hatred in my heart started melting.

After breakfast and more conversation, we went back upstairs. Mianya and I got in the bed again for a nap before really starting the day. I had a feeling Mimi wasn't going straight to sleep, though. I was right.

"Why'd you lie, Dahni? You know you're not doing anything today and you're not playing anywhere tonight." She knew my schedule.

"I know. I just didn't feel like being in my old drunk-a-lunk drill sergeant's company. I told you I didn't have the best time with her."

## Don't Ask, Don't Tell

"You don't have to go if you don't want to go." Mimi looked at me. "We can just go get some dinner and hang out downtown. I understand if you don't want to go over there."

"Don't you wanna hang with your friends, Mimi? Just go. I'll go back to the room."

"No, you're not. I can hang with them anytime. There's no telling the next time I'll get you out this way." *You do have a point, sister.*

"I'll go with you over there, Mimi. You're fun and full of surprises this weekend. "Mimi?"

"Yes?"

"Why didn't you tell me that you mess with girls?"

*

Mianya looked at me with very kind eyes and said, "I date women and I didn't tell you because it was none of your business, Dahni."

Okay, then!

"I'm not trying to be smart, sweetie. For real. I didn't know you like that. All I knew was you were a quiet twenty year old that kept to herself but seemed to be cool. Once I figured out you were real and true and that you had my back, I also figured out that you were a sort of homo/hetero phobe. I mean, you don't deal with anyone. Just your guy friends and me--in the room only. I didn't know how to take you."

"So you figured you just spring the shit on me and see if I exploded, huh? That was a great idea."

"Shush it. After I got to know you and we had been around each other for a few months, I knew what I could get away with as far as you're concerned."

"Oh, really?"

"So I took a chance, D, and I was right."

"If I hadda snapped out on your ass you woulda been sorry!"

She laughed. "I really would have. But something in me knew that you were gonna be OK. I mean, you're a really good person all the way through. I knew you wouldn't trip like that." I was lying on my back now. She moved toward me and put her head on my chest. I put my arm around her. Things were kinda cool.

"Mianya, what did your friend mean by she heard so much about me?" I felt her start smiling.

"Nothing. She's a busybody who's always trying to keep shit going." Mianya giggled to herself and I laughed because I knew she was just saying that shit.

"Do you talk about me to your friends?" She lifted up her head and looked at me.

"Nobody's spending their days discussing the great Dahni McPhail, honey. Don't even get your mind all gassed up. I just let my friends know I had a cool roommate. That's all." She put her head back down on my chest but I could still feel her giggling, laughing, or something.

"Yeah, right"

"Mimi?"

"What, McPhail?"

"Will you please not do me like that again, ever? I mean throwing shit on me. Just tell me. Whatever is going on, give me the opportunity to say yes or no. I would like a choice next time." She lifted her head again and looked at me. I could see she was sincere.

"OK, Dahni. I'm sorry. I won't do you like that again. I'll always ask you first from here on out. I promise." She kissed me on the lips and laid her head back on my chest. Was it me, or was something *happening*? That was my last thought as I fell asleep.

*

"You clean up good, Dahni." Mianya made these googly eyes at me as I came down the stairs into the living room again.

"Whatever, crazy. You look half-way decent." Lies. Mimi never looked anything but great all the time. Even in uniform. "What time are we getting out of here?"

"Now! Come on y'all." Trish answered that for me and was walking to the door motioning at us to hurry up. There was only Mianya, Me, Trish and Diana. Di was Trish's girlfriend. She was so pretty to me. She looked like a blond haired, blue-eyed angel but she had olive skin. Her eyes were for real blue, not contacts. She said she was Italian.

"Let's ride." We were going to The Jackal's house.

We got in Trish's BMW and arrived at the Jackal's crib where it seemed like everything was in full swing. I thought they were supposed to just be watching movies? "Do you guys party like this every weekend, Mimi?"

"Pretty much. We just do it at different houses. Next weekend we're going to be in Mannheim. Are you coming with me, Dahni?" I looked at Mianya's little short five foot four ass. I hoped she could see the "hell no" written across my face. I was only there because she wanted me to be. And something inside me needed to see Sealyn. "Are you going to come with me, Dahni?"

"Miyana, are they gonna dance in here today? I brought my Ipod with me." Quick subject change.

"Once we start drinking, they'll probably move the furniture and get it started." Good. She took the bait.

We walked through the yard saying hi and went into the house to greet everyone else. One thing I can say about houses in Germany. They look plain on the outside but are extremely fly on the inside. Marble floors, vaulted ceilings, lofts, and large picturesque windows. This one was no exception. The TV *was* playing a movie. I guess that's what they meant by watching movies, but lots of other things were going on. I greeted the hosts and presented them with a case. Mom said to never go to anyone's house empty handed. "Drill, I mean, T, this is a nice place."

"Thanks, McPhail. Hey, what the hell is your first name McPhail?"

"Dahni." Meekly stated.

"Dahni???" She turned around and looked at Sealyn. "Alright, well welcome. Eat and drink as much as you want. We have the movie playing. We're about to turn on some music. Oh shit! You're a DJ, Dahni. Hey, DJ Dahni!" She thought she was being original. "You got something with you? Put it on!" I started to relax.

"Alright, T. Show me where. I'll put something on so we can get crunk."

"Mimi!"

"Here's your backpack, Dahni." I looked at her and laughed.

# Dahni McPhail

"How'd you even know I was going to ask for that?" I set up the sounds and put on some "before you really start partying" music. I walked around talking to people who were drinking, laughing or eating. All women again. Everyone was doing their own thing. Either playing cards, or dominos or a game. There was plenty going on everywhere. I went out back for a minute.

Sealyn came out in the back yard and found me. She grabbed my hand and said, "Come here. I have a surprise for you." I got that old familiar feeling at the touch of her hand. She pulled me toward the front room and said, "Come on!" What the fuck was it now?

Why did Sanders' ass walk through the door? "Ooooooooohhhhhh Shit! My mutha fuckin dawg!" We were both screaming. Sealyn kept us in the dark about the fact that we'd both be at the party. So neither of us knew what the surprise was going to be.

"Damn, dawg. I can't believe this shit!" Sanders was loud as hell. We were hugging like crazy. "I know it's about to be some serious partying up in here today!" I gave my dawg some dap.

Sanders and I brought each other up to date on everything that we had done since we'd last seen each other. She was stationed in Wiesbaden. She was just down for the weekend too.

"Sanders, give me your cell, work number, home address, blood type."

## Don't Ask, Don't Tell

We were laughing and joking. So very happy. It was great to see my friend. My numero uno homie. I told Sanders about my roommate and how she tricked me into coming out here.

"Mimi is your roommate? Everybody wants a piece of that ass. *Ev-ry-bo-ty* wants Mimi and she ain't giving up shit. She doesn't talk to anybody, period. You're the roommate, huh?"

"Yeah, and her little funny ass tricked me into coming out here this weekend. She better be glad I like her!"

"Dahni, you gotta stop saying that shit if you're gonna be around family. That's offensive."

"What? What did I say?"

"When you say things like 'funny and dyke.' That's the hateful shit that straight people say to us." Us? Did Sanders just say "us"? "Stop saying that shit, Dahni."

"You act like you're one of them or something, Sanders. What gives?"

"Fool, *you're* one of 'them.' You're just in denial, shit. Shut up for now. I want you to meet somebody." Sanders walked over to a Hispanic chick with an hourglass figure. "Dahni, this is my wife, Sabrina. Bri, this is my friend Dahni I was telling you about. The one that we had to save T from killing when we were in basic." I said hi to Bri, but I was still stuck on that word wife. I had to talk to Sanders' ass later about that and some more shit.

## Chapter 11

*Ain't no party like a Dahni Mac party!* I tell you what, I was having more fun this weekend than I'd had the whole year I'd been in Germany. So much that I was starting to change my mind about going to Mannheim with Mimi the next weekend.

"I see you're enjoying yourself." Mimi walked up behind me and whispered in my ear. I turned around to her.

"Yeah, yeah Mimi-ness. I'm having fun. Thanks for bringing me. You want me to kiss your ass now?" She looked at me and raised her right eyebrow. Damn, that was so cute.

"Don't let your mouth write a check that you can't cash, Dahni." Why does everybody have all these aphorisms?

I wanted to ask her what she meant but I said, "Whatever. I'm having an extra blast because my sister from basic training is here. She's with her 'wife' though. Whatever's up with that shit."

"Dahni, shut it up. They're in love and it doesn't matter what their gender is."

"I know. I was just surprised. Can I be surprised? Damn. I haven't seen her in I don't know how long and then when I do see her, that's what she told me. She is fully lesbianized." Mimi looked at me in a way that made me shut up. I went over to sit by Sanders and her "wife." Mimi followed me and sat down on my lap.

"You're not light, girl. You're not made of feathers."

"Be quiet, Dahni. Stop talking please because you're going to make me need a drink already today. Does your friend look happy?" I turned and looked at Sanders and Bri. They did look very, very happy. They were talking with everyone around them but you could tell that they were all about being with each other. It looked nice. "Wouldn't you like to be in a relationship with someone you care a lot about and who cares a lot about you—-regardless of what their gender is?"

"Well, my family will trip."

"Well, you're an adult and you are making your own decisions, aren't you?" *Feisty!* I was trying to figure out what the hell was going on inside Mianya's head. She was working her way toward something. Just then, I

## Don't Ask, Don't Tell

looked up and Sanders was smiling at me, mouthing the words "Is that you, dawg?" Sanders was asking me if Mimi was my girlfriend. My girlfriend? I mouthed the words, "Hell no. I'm straight." Sanders just laughed.

Just then, Sealyn walked up to us. "You ladies want to play a game? Come on, let's play." A few of us went into the dining room to play. We all sat around the table. Sealyn pulled out several different bottles of liquor and put them on the table. "You can pick your own poison. We're gonna play dirty hearts." I started getting up from the table. Mimi grabbed my arm.

"Where are you going, punk? You afraid to play?" *Afraid wasn't the word.* The last time I played that bullshit, my whole world changed.

"I don't want to play. These games are too personal."

"Aw, come on and play. It's just a game." Everyone at the table was trying to get me to join in. "What? Am I going to find out something you don't want me to know?" Mimi asked me that and I almost looked up at Sealyn but I maintained control over my head's reaction.

I covered up by saying, "I told y'all mutha fuggas I ain't never skurred!" Everybody laughed. I sat back down to play. *Oh, I was scared.* I was more than scared. Fuckin' Sealyn. She knew what she was doing.

Mimi got me a beer before the game started. When she did that, I thought about how Mianya was really taking care of me and making sure

## Dahni McPhail

I was comfortable that weekend. I knew Mimi but I didn't know the extent of how friendly and nice she was. She was ideal. I mean, for someone who was into women.

The cards went around once and Sanders got a heart. "Sanders, have you ever been with anyone in this room besides your girlfriend?" Oh, these women were starting off deep from the jump. I turned up my beer so I could numb my nerves and get ready for the ride. Sanders took a minute to answer. I was like, what the hell? Had Sanders been with more people in the room than the girl she was with?

Then she answered, "Yeah. I stuck Dahni in the ass when we were in basic."

"You's a damn lie!" I yelled. Everybody laughed. Mianya looked at me.

"Mimi, Sanders is playing. We never got down like that. She was too busy kissing on that other girl. I forgot her name." Why did I feel the need to explain myself?

"Well who were you kissing on, Dahni?"

"Get a heart and ask me, Mianya. Play the game and stop breaking the rules. You're breaking the rules, girl!" Everybody laughed again.

Bri said, "Dahni, you have a heart." *FUCK ME!!!* I didn't even want to look up and see Mianya's mouth forming the words.

139

## Don't Ask, Don't Tell

Then I heard, "Dahni, have you ever been in love?" It was Sealyn. Why in the world would she ask me some shit like that publicly? Fucking females.

I pondered on my response, and then I answered. "I thought I was in love but I realized that I was in love by myself. I was naïve and dumb and basically got my heart broken by some liar who was more experienced than me and just wanted to fuck me and fuck with my head." *Now, where the hell did all that come from?* Mimi looked at me as I glared at Sealyn. Everything got quiet for a moment. Then, the game continued.

I didn't answer any more questions after that. I just took shots. The other players got tired of asking me and started directing questions to everyone else. As the drinking continued, the dares started getting funnier and funnier. We were being stupid as hell and I was having a blast. Then, Mimi got another heart and Sanders jumped at the opportunity.

"Mimi, I dare you to kiss Dahni for one minute." I looked at Sanders and my look told her that I would be dealing with her later for this mutha fuggin' bull shit!

"Kiss me? For a whole minute!" I screamed. "In front of all these people," I thought.

"Stop acting like a punk, McPhail." The Jackal had to open her freaking mouth. I'd almost forgotten she was there.

"I don't know." I looked down at the floor.

"Y'all don't have to do it in front of us. Go in the bathroom!" I was really, really hoping that Sanders' buzzed no, drunk ass would shut the hell up.

"You don't have to, Dahni. But take a shot." Mimi gave me an out. I took the shot. Sealyn must have been tipsy because her loud ass thought she was whispering when she said, "I see ain't nothing changed." And Mianya heard every word she said.

I left the game after that and went into the room to pump up the music. I put on one of my party playlists and started dancing by myself. I was trying to come down from my five million shots. I was out there for a minute and in my own world. When I looked up, the floor was packed. I guess everyone else decided to come in and party with me. Sanders was out there kicking it with Bri. I gave Sanders some dap. That was when I noticed Sanders was doing the lead thing. The boy/girl thing. Dominant. Sanders was the dominant person in the relationship. I committed that to memory and kept dancing. When I looked up, Mianya was in front of me. I turned around and Sealyn was behind me. I looked at Sanders and that asshole was laughing. She was the only one there who knew all my secrets. She seemed to know something about Sealyn as well. Sanders was enjoying my pain to the max. Regardless, I couldn't let these chicks out dance me. I had to break them off.

Both of them came in really close to me and worked my body with their bodies. That's when I realized that both of them were tore out of the frame. **Fucked up!** …And being nasty. A voice in my head said, "*I wonder what it would be like in bed with these two…*" OK, hearing the drunk Dahni voice confirmed that I was lit too. But they felt so damn good against me. Work dat shyt! I turned around toward Mimi and she came close to me. When Mimi came close, Sealyn came close on my backside. I was getting horny. I started popping and dancing around so they would back up off me.

Then I turned around to face Sealyn. She came up to me and put her arms around my neck. I put my hands around her waist. We were face-to-face, drunk, and instantly forgetting about everyone else in the room. It seemed like everything around us blacked out and we were the only two on the dance floor and the only two on earth. Fucked up and fucking up! She put her nose on mine and I felt a kiss coming on when. . .

"Can I cut in?" Trish broke up the whole scenario.

I backed up and said, "Sure." I didn't know that Trish was saving my drunk ass and Sealyn's. The Jackal hadn't seen the vertical make out session. I regrouped, backed up and turned around to continue dancing with Mianya. She was nowhere to be found.

\*

I left the dance floor to go and find Mimi. As I left, I saw Sanders laughing her ass off. I'm glad she was enjoying this shit. Mimi was out in the back yard again, drinking something. "Mimi." She just sat there. "Mimi! Mianya!" I walked over and sat in the chair next to her.

"What, Dahni?" She said "what" so hard, she spat.

"What's wrong with you? Why'd you leave?" She turned and looked at me. She stared and didn't say a word. "Mimi, are you drunk?"

"Asshole, hell yeah I'm fucked up but that doesn't mean I'm crazy or blind. You's a liar. You are a liar, Dahni McPhail. You and Sealyn have or had something going on!" I looked around to see if anyone could hear this woman with her loud ass self. Drunk and mad does not a good combination make.

"You wanna go somewhere else and talk?" I was trying to get her away from the female ears with their fucking internal recording devices.

"No. I don't. You don't want anybody to hear your shit, Dahni? Huh? Straight motherfucker! You don't want to get busted out?" Now it was time to get this chick to a secure environment before she said some shit that neither one of us could recover from.

Pissed, I snatched her ass up and took her out front to the car. "Get in."

"Fuck you, McPhail!"

"What the hell is wrong with you, Mianya? What's going on?"

"You're a liar. That's what's wrong with me." What the?

## Don't Ask, Don't Tell

"*I'm a liar, bitch?*" *My mouth spoke before my mind thought.* "You're the one who brought me out here to this bullshit in the first place! Were you honest about that?" Silence. Her eyes pierced mine and I fully expected a slap.

"What did you just call me, Dahni?" I immediately tried to apologize but she snatched away from me and walked back into the house and into the bathroom. I caught her just before she closed the bathroom door. I went in and closed the door behind me.

"I'm sorry, Mianya! I'm sorry. That just came out."

"Asshole, you need to just come the fuck out!" *Oh my goodness.* "That's what your got damn problem is!" She was all up in my face now. The little church mouse was mad as hell. Why did I start laughing? I mean, I just fell out laughing. "That's your damn problem, Dahni. Everything is a joke!"

"Mianya, how many problems do I have? I need to come out. That's my problem. I don't even know what I need to come out of. I think everything is a joke. That's my problem." I continued to laugh. She couldn't stay mad at me because I was too stupid. I couldn't stop laughing. She started laughing too.

"Dahni, stop. You make me sick! I can't stand you!"

"Well, I'm just trying to get some information, Mianya. You're the one storming out of rooms, screaming, and telling me what I need to do and all that shit. Help me to understand." She laughed a little longer and then got serious and put her finger in my face.

"Call me another bitch as long as you live, hear?"

"I'm sorry, Mimi. For real."

Then she grabbed my hands, looked into my eyes and said, "Dahni, please just tell me the truth. Please. What's up with you and Sealyn?"

The way Mianya looked at me made me melt. Why was she so very interested in this Sealyn stuff? Why did it even matter to her? Why was it so important? "Mianya, I—" BOOM! BOOM! BOOM!

"Other people have to use the bathroom, you know!"

"Sorry!" I started moving toward the door to open it. Mianya grabbed my arm and turned me to her.

"Are you going to tell me?"

"I promise you. I'm going to tell you, Sealyn. I mean. . ."

I thought she looked at me crazy earlier. If you could have seen the look in Mimi's eyes when that name came out of my mouth! She pushed me out of the way. I almost fell in the bathtub. Then she stormed out of the bathroom. "Trish, I'm ready to go!" she screamed. And the party was over for me that night.

## Don't Ask, Don't Tell

Mianya didn't say one single word to me on the way back to Trish's apartment. She didn't say a word when we went to sleep, when we woke up, got dressed, rode back to the dorms, or when we got in our room. The chick was pissed off at Dahni McPhail. There was no talking to her.

So, I just stretched out on my bed and put on my headphones. No use in trying to make conversation. I felt my cell phone vibrate and answered it. It was Sanders. "What up, baller?"

"Whatever, Sanders. What's up?"

"I'm just calling to check on you and to see how you're doing. I know you're in the dog house."

"Sanders, my room mate is crazy."

"Keep my name out of your mouth!" Mianya shouted over the wall lockers. Damn near 24 hours and that's all she could say to me. I got up and walked out the room.

"Sanders, talk to me and tell me what's going on, please."

"Dahni, you ain't that damn stupid. Mianya likes you, fool. You are all she ever, EVA talks about. She won't talk to anyone because she is waiting for your dumb ass."

"Well, I can't help her. I'm straight."

"Whatever, Dahni. Anyway, let me tell you about the latest Sealyn shit." Sanders told me that Sealyn was still feeling me. Sealyn's point of view was that I refused to deal with her because I'm straight, in my mind, and I'm ashamed of our relationship.

"What? That lying bitch. Sanders, I was starting to feel her and she fucking slept with me one night when we were at training on pass, and then she left without saying shit. The next time I see Sealyn, she's with the Jackal and at the same time I find out that the Jackal is who she's been with all along. How the fuck am I to blame?"

"Well dog, she said she left you some kind of letter and you ignored it."

"She's lying. She didn't leave me a letter."

"Well, all I can say is your issue is *really* bad. *Woe is Dahni!* You have two fine ass females in love with you. I feel sorry for you."

"You ain't gotta be sarcastic, Sanders. I need you to be serious right now."

"All right. Well you can at least do something about one issue. Just go and talk to Mianya. At least she's single and she loves you whether you know it or not. Say something to her."

"Say what? 'I want a lesbian relationship with you, Mianya?' Fuck that. I'll holla at you later."

I got back to the room and Mianya was coming out the door with her bag packed. "Where are you going?"

"None of your straight, wrong name calling, lying ass business. I'm moving out. I'm going to talk to billeting in the morning. Bye." I stood in the doorway and watched as Mianya's heels clicked down the hall.

"You need to stop acting crazy." I screamed behind her.

"Shut up, McPhail!" She sounded like she was crying.

*

The next morning, Mianya came in, got her things and moved out just like she said she would. I felt like someone had taken an anvil and dropped it on my head. I couldn't believe she would do this to me. She was tripping entirely too hard over nothing. What was her problem with Sealyn anyway? Mianya and I certainly weren't together, plus none of this girl on girl stuff is actually a real relationship. It's just something everyone was doing until they find a husband! Her leaving was real as a motherfucker, though.

## Chapter 12

I got back into the groove of hanging out with my boys, DJing, and just chilling by myself. I hadn't seen Mimi in weeks. Sanders and I hung out now a little bit. Since we were in different cities, we couldn't roll every day. But we managed to fit in some weekends.

"Dahni are you ever going to talk to Mianya?"

"I wasn't the one who stopped talking to her, Sanders. Mianya is on some other shit. She got mad because I made a simple mistake. Then she went and moved out. She took it there, not me. What can I do about that?"

"Well, have you talked to Sealyn about anything?"

"Nope. All I've been doing is working out, djing and running with my boys. Chilling in my room. Nothing more and nothing less. Plus Sealyn isn't the problem."

# Don't Ask, Don't Tell

"You need to quit it, Dahni and talk to Mimi..."

Quit what? In my mind, I wasn't doing anything. Sanders needed to quit talking to me about all this bull shit. Mimi hadn't spoken to me in over a month. She was really done with me. It hurt but I had to keep living. So, I focused on me and my career, and my DJing and basketball skills. Basketball.

That's how I met Michael Friday. I'd seen him around the Kaserne here and there and a few times when I was hanging around with my boys Krys and Adrian so I recognized his face when he came up to me on the court in the gym.

"That's a nice three you got. You play ball in school?"

Michael was actually a good looking guy. He smiled at me with a set of beautiful teeth, accented by a chip in his right incisor. He looked around 6 feet tall, and carried 180 pounds of pure muscle like most Army guys. He was a hot boy by any standard and he was a great basketball player on top of that.

"Yeah, dude." I started walking toward my gym bag.

"Let's play some "horse." You got time for a game?

I turned around and looked at him. He was smiling again. This time I noticed his grey eyes. He was standing with his hands on his hips, one hand holding the basketball to the side.

"You know you're not doing anything. You're down here almost every day by yourself playing ball. Play a game with me. What's your name?"

"My name is "I prefer not to be stalked." I grabbed up my bag and headed out the door.

"My name is Mike!" he screamed after me.

I kept walking.

I left the gym perturbed at the fact this fool had been watching me like a maniac. I walked into my room, slammed my door and got into the shower. Tonite was my first night DJing at the noncommissioned officer club and I needed to have my head straight so that I could make a good impression. I wanted to keep this job because it paid two hundred and fifty dollars per night. I liked that kind of chump change. I thought about whether Sanders was gonna make it to my show tonite. She usually came up to see Bri on the weekends regardless of whether our paths crossed or not. I called her cell to make sure she was gonna come out and hang with me while I was playing.

"What up, Sanders? What you getting into tonite?"

"I'm in town with Bri now. I'm dropping her off and coming over to the club to hang with you later but I have a few things to do first. What you been up to, Dahni with your absent ass? Man, you and Mimi need to stop tripping, dude. Are you ever going to talk to Mianya?"

## Don't Ask, Don't Tell

"San, are you gonna say the same thing every time I talk to you? I wasn't the one who stopped talking to her, Sanders. Mianya is on some other shit. She just got mad because I didn't want to freak with her full time and blamed it on the fact I called her Sealyn by mistake. I was drunk, dude. Then she moved out. I didn't tell her to leave. What can I do about that? Plus I met this guy I like anyway."

There I went with the embellishments again, knowing that I just met this dude, and wasn't really interested. Even worse, knowing that by saying it, I was going to have to show and prove when it came to Sanders.

"You're a damn lie, Dahni. You ain't meet nobody. Call Mimi, man. Y'all so fuckin' dramatic!"

"I'm for real, San. I met some dude named Mike. He might be at the party tonight." Lies. All lies.

"Aiite, man. Whatever you say. I'll be at the club tho. We can get it in tonite because we can walk from the club back to your room, Dahni. Can't catch a case for stumbling back to your room on foot."

"And you know this, San! I'll see you out there! Thanks for supporting me, punk."

"Whatever!"

It's amazing how a lie can become the truth. The party at the club started at 9. Sanders got there about 9:30 and Mike walked up to the DJ booth at about 9:45. That's what you call perfect timing.

"What's up DJ? You do it all, huh? Breaking ankles on the court, DJing and a super Soldier. How can you be all these things?"

Mike was smiling at me with that silly but cute grin.

"Why are you investigating me? What did you say your name was again?"

I actually remembered that his name was Mike. For some reason, he'd stayed on my mind after the gym conversation. It wasn't a good or a bad feeling. The feeling was strange.

"Mike is my name. Staff Sergeant Michael Friday. I work over in 89th Transportation Brigade. Don't you remember me? You come over to my building every Wednesday for the administration meeting."

I guess I had tunnel vision because I thought I only knew him from basketball. I didn't remember seeing him there.

"I'm Dahni. This is my friend San."

San gave him the dirtiest of dirty looks. That wasn't a good sign. "Sup," she dryly offered, chucked him two sticks then turned toward me and started talking like he wasn't there.

"You know this nigga right here ain't shit, number one. Number two, you know you need to call Mimi."

## Don't Ask, Don't Tell

San came to that conclusion about Mike because, simply, he was a guy. The fact that he was handsome made him a whore and no good in her mind. As far as I saw, the only bad thing about him was the grey eyes but that was because of previous experiences with our crazy ass drill sergeant. He was sweet. Dark chocolate with curly hair, finely sculpted eyebrows and long eye lashes—so long that you could tell as soon as he blinked. He knew how to dress and was a young Staff Sergeant, doing very well in his career. I really couldn't see anything wrong with him, but San could.

"He's a whore. Every time I see him, he's with a different girl, Dahni."

"So, San. What does that have to do with me at this point? I'm not trying to marry him. I just met the dude."

"A-hem." Mike interrupted our conversation.

San and I turned toward Mike.

"Um, I know I can't ask you to dance but can I get both of you something to drink or something to eat or both?"

And he was a gentleman. My mother would be so very happy. Maybe I could at least have a conversation every once in a while with the guy. What would it hurt?

"Thanks. Can you get us both a shot of Patron and a Heffeweizen, some Soldier Wings and fries with cheddar cheese and turkey bacon on them? Small, please? Thank you."

San placed the order for us. As he walked away, she turned toward me again.

"Yes, Dahni. That bitch will pay for our attention and for yours. Make sure you tap the ATM. Get something for your time."

I laughed. I could tell that San might be softening up. That was her way of authorizing me to hang out with him for a minute.

San relented. "He's cute, Dahni. He's a lil' handsome "hard leg" but is this what you really want to do? Are you sure you're just not hurt over you and Mimi?"

"San, the only thing I have experienced since I've messed with women is pain and drama. I'm not built for that bullshit. I'd rather date him and not ride the emotional roller coaster. At least I know all he is gonna be is a man. We all know what comes with that. Women come with daggers aimed straight at your heart, disguised with sweetness. I don't even think they know it's in their nature. They just hurt you for no reason. I don't want to deal with that craziness anymore. I want a family. Plus, I can take him home if it comes down to it."

"Yeah, take me home. I'm great boyfriend material. Parents love me!"

"Dang, you're all in our conversation!" San was indignant. "Why you sneaking up on people, dude. What's up with that?"

That was some stealth shit. He just popped the hell up. Even San didn't hear him and San never misses anything.

## Don't Ask, Don't Tell

"I'm Dahni, Mike. I don't remember if I told you my name or not." I reached out to shake his hand and met a strong hand with beautifully manicured fingers adorned with diamond filled platinum rings. Was that a Rolex on his arm? This was a bit over the top but I can understand grandeur. I like flyness.

"Nice to officially meet you. How about that game of "horse" tomorrow?"

"Sure."

We played the game and after he cheated and beat me by one point…

"Nah, DeeDee. You know you're wrong. I didn't cheat!" he chuckled with that cheeky grin.

Mike and I started spending quite a bit of time together. We both were interested in music and photography. We liked to cook and visit different restaurants and eat where the locals suggested. We both loved to party and get fucked up. We really had a lot of the same interests. Now that I knew who he was, I realized that we did have to attend many of the same meetings and military functions because our higher headquarters was the same. So, nowadays I did notice that he was almost everywhere I was.

"You mean all this time, you never saw me in any of these meetings or events, DeeDee?"

"No. I never saw you."

"DeeDee" is his affectionate name for me. I couldn't tell him that I wasn't even looking at men period, much less him. He was used to attention because of his pretty boy thing but he was a member of the male species. At the time he was checking me out, my eyes were following tits and ass. Actually, they still did. Mike was starting to notice that more too. One day we were in my room taking Patron shots and playing table football with "Set it off" on the TV. He made a face at the Queen and finally spoke.

"DeeDee, I heard that you used to mess around with females. Is that true?"

"Here we go. Go somewhere with that shit, man. Let's take a double shot. Why is that of any interest to you?" My mouth was reckless.

"You talk to me any kind of way, girl. I was just wondering. I mean, we're cool now right and we've been chilling for a minute. Like two months, really. I thought we could talk about it."

"Mike, one of the things you'll find about me is that I don't discuss things that are not relevant to my current situation. Meaning, it ain't got nothing to do with us now so I don't wish to discuss it."

"I was just asking. I want to know everything about you. I really like you."

"I like you too man, but dredging up unfounded stories doesn't do anything for our situation. It's not important."

## Don't Ask, Don't Tell

"Can I ask you something else?" Mike was persistent.

I started to wonder was it the movie that was making him ask the lesbianized questions or was he going around asking or inquiring about me. He was always telling me something about myself that I never remembered telling him. I needed to figure out what really was going on.

"If its personal, don't ask me, Mike."

"Its personal but it's not the same type of question. Are we ever going to hug or kiss or have sex?"

Awwwwwww fuck! I forgot the nigga had a dick and would probably be asking me about sex eventually. Damn, and we've been chillin' for two months so we were in the time frame.

"I'm not ready for sex Mike. I don't want to kiss you. I don't feel I've known you long enough for that and if that's what you're here for you need to go head on, dude, cause you have the wrong female. I'm not trying to get down with you."

"Damn, DeeDee. You don't want to kiss me? You don't even like me?"

He looked like I hurt his feelings but I really couldn't help him with that. My mind was definitely not on sex. Not with him.

"I didn't mean it like that." Realizing my words were rather harsh. "I like you. You're nice. You're cool. We have fun. You're a great friend."

"Well, I love you and you don't even seem to care, DeeDee. All you do is sit around and look at that picture of ole girl over there. Who is she anyway?"

"My cousin. She died in a stripper pole accident."

"You're lying. I've seen her around here."

"Well, why did you ask then, bitch?" I caught fire immediately when it came to Mianya!

"I said don't fucking ask me questions. Bye. Get the fuck out. Take your ass home then." I was livid.

How the fuck was he gonna be snooping around in my business asking me about Mimi? Time to go, boy. I got up and walked toward the door. Mike jumped up, ran behind me and grabbed both my arms.

"Why are you so mad? Is it because you really are gay. Are you gay, DeeDee? Just tell me, please. I love you anyway. I want to marry you anyway. Please tell me. We can work through anything. I just don't want to be in the dark. I can deal with anything that you tell me. I just need you to be honest. I want to know where I stand!"

Mike looked at me, his eyes filling with tears. "I just want to know where I stand, DeeDee. I love you."

When did we get to love? How did he get from like to love in one conversation? Why did he look sincere? There was actually something that seemed to resemble love in this set of grey eyes. Fuck. This dude really loves me. Wow.

I hugged him. He kissed me.

I sighed and looked at the floor.

He apologized.

"Man, I'll holla at you later." I opened the door to let him out.

Mike grabbed his back pack and his things and headed out the door. "I really love you, DeeDee."

"Aiite, Dude."

I closed the door and leaned against it, listening as Mike walked down the hall away from my room. I went over to the window and watched him walk down the street until he was out of sight. His conversation had me in deep thought. I was so restless. I felt bad for him because I really liked him but I refused to lie to him about my feelings. He didn't deserve for me to lie and say I loved him when I didn't.

"Fuck it all, you Warriors!" I quoted my old drill sergeant then I grabbed my basketball and headed down to the park to shoot some hoops to clear my mind. As I got closer to the park, I saw a couple of chicks sitting on the bench chilling. They were directly in my path to the courts. They looked kind of familiar and as I walked up to them, I realized why. It was Mimi and the new Sergeant in my unit. What the fuck was Mimi doing with her? The Sergeant reached over and pulled Mimi to her, kissing her softly on the lips. I froze in my tracks. I couldn't move. I dropped my basketball to the ground which made Mimi jump to her feet.

"Dahni!"

My heart dropped to my feet and my anger rose to the crown of my head. Skank ass, BITCH!!!! THAT BITCH! That's why she wasn't talking to me! I turned around and ran as fast as I could straight to Michael's dorm room. I banged on his door like a crazy person.

He answered wearing only his ball shorts and his creamy cocoa skin. I threw my arms around his neck so he could not see my face.

"I love you, Mike! I do love you."

"Really? You love me?"

"Yes, I cried into his shoulder."

"I want to marry you DeeDee!"

I didn't say anything. He shut the door. I let him pick me up and carry me over to his bed. He placed me on the bed and I quickly turned off the lights, hopefully hiding the feelings on my face.

"I love you so much."

I heard Michael in the distance telling me all the things so many other women would kill to hear coming from his mouth to their ears.

# Don't Ask, Don't Tell

"I want to spend the rest of my life with you, DeeDee."

"OK."

That's what I said, but all I could see was Mimi kissing that Sergeant on the park bench.

"I love you Mimi." I guess he thought I called him Mikey.

"I promise I won't hurt you or break your heart, he breathed." Michael began kissing my lips. We kissed for what seemed like hours before he advanced to my neck. He trembled as his hands gently removed my wife beater and my bra. I raised up to help him remove the rest of my clothes. His grey eyes pierced through the darkness looking at me for signs of love. I pulled his lips to mine, kissing him softly. I slid my tongue into his mouth exploring his tongue with my tongue. I took his tongue into my mouth and sucked it forcefully back and forth. He pulled away.

"Damn. Nobody's...."

I grabbed the back of his head and pulled his mouth to mine again dominating his mouth with mine. I flipped him over on his back and placed my naked body on top of his. My pussy rested on his stomach. His nature began to rise against my buttocks. I kissed and sucked his neck, rubbing my face into the smoothness of his skin. He always smelled so good. Further I went. I kissed his chest and squeezed his nipples between my forefingers and thumbs. They were hard as little pebbles. His breathing quickened. He seemed a little confused by my aggressiveness so I helped him out and put his hands on my waist and moved them. He got the idea and began to caress my body. I bit down on his nipple hard and he moaned.

"Shit!"

I bit his right nipple even harder, flicking my tongue over it at the same time. His hands gripped me tighter. I could tell by the bulge in his shorts that he was working with some equipment and when I licked my way down his stomach and pulled down his shorts, his dick was eight inches long and as thick as my forearm. I licked and bit his thighs making note of his cleanly shaven area. He moved his hips toward my mouth. I licked my hand and caressed his dick, working my hand up and down his shaft. He got harder and harder. I climbed up his body again and kissed his pretty mouth.

"Come on…"

He followed my command and I pulled him to the middle of the bed I spread his legs, grabbed his dick and squeezed it hard. He winced in pain but quickly changed his mourn to a moan when I placed my lips over the tip of his cock and rimmed it with my tongue. His dick bounced and throbbed at the attention I was giving it. I moved my body around so that my pussy was in his face.

"Lick it."

## Don't Ask, Don't Tell

I spread my legs and put my pussy directly on his lips. His tongue shot out and his lips enveloped my labia. I had to give him an "e" for effort. I deep throated his phallus and his hips jerked like he was about to come. I pulled away from him and laid with him face to face.

"I love you so much, Dahni." I tongue kissed the hell out of him to shut him up.

"Show me you love me. Where are your condoms?" I pulled a rubber out of his night stand drawer and gently placed it on his rock hard dick. I was a little intimidated by the size of the dong being that I'd never had anything that big, but I figured that was nothing a little KY jelly and some determination couldn't fix. I grabbed the lube and covered his phallus with it, then I smothered my pussy completely, inside and out. "Get your pussy, Mikey."

He put the tip of his cock on my clit and I could feel its burning heat. It throbbed as he moved it downward, searching for my syrupy canal. He pushed forward and his magnificent dick slowly invaded my tight walls. Inch by inch he spread me open. I had to catch my breath and relax my muscles. The nigga was so big, I never thought he would be completely inside but at last I felt his balls rest against me. I bit down into his shoulder and grabbed his ass cheeks, making him work his cock inside my pussy. His stomach jerked and his breathing quickened.

"Don't come. I thought you wanted to fuck me?"

"I do. I want to give you all this dick." He lifted my legs over his shoulders putting me in the buck and drove himself deeper and deeper inside me. Every thrust felt like the first one each time his large pole reentered and exited and reentered. He pulled out and grabbed me up and put me on my knees. I looked back at him as he positioned himself. Then, he drove his dick inside me slowly and forcefully. He lifted his leg up leaned over my back and grabbed my nipples, pinching them while he rode my pussy. I wrapped my legs around his back and we flipped over. He ended up on his back with me riding on top of his dick. I was looking at his well groomed feet. I don't know what made me bust this next move but it just came into my mind all of a sudden. Probably the years of gay porn. I spread his legs open as I rode him, reached under his balls and slid my middle finger inside his asshole. Michael yelled my name out loud and started fucking the life out of me. I pounded his asshole with my finger until I heard the unmistakable sound of him busting a nut. He jerked uncontrollably as I finger fucked him with everything I had. After a few more gyrations, he took a deep breath and lay flat on his back breathing deeply. I slid my finger out of his ass, got up and went to the bathroom to wash up. When I came back to lay next to him, he kissed me softly on the lips and asked me,

"What made you do that to me?"

"I don't even know. I'm sorry about that."

"I never did that before. I'm so in love with you."

I kissed him. "I know Mike."

## Don't Ask, Don't Tell

I lay close to him and went to sleep. I closed my eyes and there was Mimi anyway.

I woke up hung over and in the bed of the man who loved me more than anything in this world. I opened my eyes to see him smiling at me with that chipped tooth.

"Hey DeeDee. Good morning." He was so happy.

"Whassup, dude." I sat up in the bed and looked around. Then I realized that I was naked. Sober, I snatched the covers over myself.

"No need in covering up now, girl. I already seen what cha workin' with!"

"Shut UP, Mike. Dang. Oh my gosh it's really not the time to be silly. Give me about forty five minutes to get it together. Give me a beer."

"You roll like a dude, DeeDee. Why do you drink like that?"

"Are you really about to start asking me questions. Yes, I gets fucked up. That's how I roll. Is it new? I'm not changing for you." I glared into his eyes to shut that shit up from the door. He looked at a bag on the desk.

"I went and got some breakfast, babe."

"Thank you."

I ate my food and I started gathering my clothes and putting them on, remembering the events that took place last night. Remembering everything that led up to me being in this room with this man in this position and state of mind. I glanced over at Mike again feeling a little weird but it was washed away by the love in his eyes and that chipped tooth grin he grinned every time I looked in his direction. I guess I needed to get used to this new relationship I'd created with this man. It's not that I didn't like Mike. It's not that I didn't love Mike. I just did not feel what he felt and there was no escaping that. But right then and there I decided that his love could be enough for us both. At least that's what it seemed like from where I was sitting.

"That was nice, Mike. I appreciate the food."

I walked over to him, kissed him and wrapped my arms around him. I felt what seemed to be a huge sigh of relief from him as he wrapped his arms around me and held me tightly.

"I have to head over to my room. I gotta run some errands." I walked over to the bed to get the rest of my things and turned up my beer.

"I can take you, DeeDee. You can take my car if you want. Here's my keys." He offered me the keys to his Land Rover.

"I'm good Mikey. Just meet me down at the gym around four so we can play some "horse." I feel like kicking your ass. Or text me, aiite? Imma get with you later."

When I got back to the room, my basketball was at my door with a note from Mimi on top of it.

## Don't Ask, Don't Tell

"You're wrong again."

I kicked the fuckin' basketball down the hall.

"Bitch!"

At this moment, I hated Mimi.

"If you break something in this hallway, you know you're going to have to pay for it." A sickeningly sweet familiarity rang in my ears.

"Sealyn!" I swung around at the sound of her voice.

"Hey Baby." She walked up to me and gave me a hug and a kiss.

"What you been getting yourself into lately? I haven't seen you in a while."

Of all the shit that I did not need in my life, Sealyn was definitely at the top of that shit list.

"Yo." That's all I could muster. I put my key into the door and turned the handle. She followed me into my room.

"What have you been up to, DeeDee?" Sealyn called me that name Mike uses.

"Shut up, Sealyn. What do you want?" Sealyn was the reason why all this shit was going on in my life anyway. I've had nothing but trouble since I met her ass.

# Dahni McPhail

"Your boyfriend is cute," she smirked.

"Shut up bitch. Damn, Sealyn!" She really was asking for it.

"Don't get mad at me because you got a man and I'm being straight up with you. Don't hide it. And I'm not your bitch either. You're my bitch if you really want to assign titles. Anyway, I just came by to tell you that I love you and I miss you."

By this time I had washed my face and brushed my teeth and readied myself for the shower.

"I love you Dahni McPhail. No matter how it seems, I am always here for you. If you have any problems, you can always call me. I have your back. There will be strings attached, bitch, cause you know I want some of that pussy but I will be there for you, aiite?"

I tried not to laugh at that girl. I really tried not to even smile. But a part of me was glad to hear Sealyn be Sealyn. So, I laughed and I laughed and I laughed like the mentally exhausted person I was.

"That's my baby. You can't hide from yourself, OK, Dahni? And you can't ever fucking hide from me as long as your ass is living and black. I am your proverbial fly on the wall, Dahni. Don't fucking play. If you need anything or if this nigga causes you any problems, baby, I will be right here just like I am today."

"Why would Mike cause me any problems, Sealyn? There you go with your riddle shit."

## Don't Ask, Don't Tell

Sealyn walked up to me and cupped my face in her soft hands. She placed her lips on mine and kissed me long and slow. She reached her hands around my head and pulled me closer to her, sliding her tongue inside my mouth, flicking her tongue on mine. I could feel the tingle between my legs as my heart started to pound. I reached forward to put my hands around her waist, she pulled away.

"You belong to me. Take care of yourself and look in the mirror, please. Stop bullshitting that girl, OK? You can fuck him all you want but you can't forget this feeling."

Sealyn smiled that beautiful smile, slapped my ass and walked out the door. All I could think about was would I ever, ever feel what she made me feel with Mike? She made me horny that fast. I went into the shower and washed off the rest of my night.

I skipped the game of horse with Mike and I didn't answer any of his calls or texts. I didn't feel like being bothered. I finally hit him up around ten that night.

"What's up, Mikey?"

"Hey." I could tell he was feeling some kind of way.

"What's wrong with you?"

"I thought you were supposed to hang out with me today. What happened?"

Oh my goodness. I know this guy wasn't really questioning me like this.

"Come on, dude. Are you serious? What did you do today?"

"Nothing. I was waiting on you to call me or at least text me like you said, so I just chilled."

"So, Mikey, you stayed in the room all day waiting on me to call you? You have a cell phone. You know you can take it with you, right? What's really going on, man?"

"I just wanted to be with you. Are you coming over, DeeDee?

"Um, no. Did I tell you that I was coming over?"

"No, you didn't tell me that. Can I come over to your room?"

Damn, I did not feel like chilling with him tonite.

"I'm not trying to have sex with you tonite, Mike."

"I just want to sleep with you. We don't have to have sex."

Is this how things were going to be now? Wasn't I supposed to be the one running behind him?

"Aiite, man. Come on over."

As soon as I hung up with Mike, Sealyn called me on the phone.

## Don't Ask, Don't Tell

"Dahni, look on your desk for me and see if you see my ID card. It's in a clear, plastic cover."

I looked on the desk and didn't see it. Then I looked on the floor.

"I see it, Sealyn. It fell between the crack on my desk."

"OK, I'm coming around the corner. I'll be up in a minute."

Sealyn came in and got her ID card. "Thanks, babe."

She kissed me again as she was walking out the door. "Call me, Dahni."

"No! Get out! Psyche. I'mma hit you up, girl." Mike was already there coming in the door after she left.

"Hey, Mikey." Sealyn sang as she sashayed past Mike and down the hallway. Mike came in and closed the door behind him.

"You hang out with her? Everybody knows she's gay, Dahni!"

"Go back to your room or mind your business," I blew him off, grabbed my remote, and bounced on my bed. Mike came around and stood in front of me.

"Are you sleeping with her, Dahni? I just want to know."

"Mike, do I ask you questions about any bitch? Do I? Don't ask me any questions, shit. You're getting on my nerves, man."

---

172

For a second, I thought I saw something recognizably crazy in Mike's grey eyes, but I knew it couldn't be that. He let out a hard sigh and plopped down beside me on my bed.

"You shouldn't be hanging around with people like that, especially her."

"I promise I won't tell you who to hang around with, ever, ok? Do me the same favor."

I kissed Mike on the cheek, turned off my lights and lay in his arms, thinking about what I thought I saw in his eyes for that fleeting moment. I felt his breathing get even, then I went to sleep.

The "Iron Might" basketball tournament was on and poppin' and our squads were in the final four. Both Mike and I played for our Post's teams and we were in the battle for the championships in the male and female categories. It was looking good for both of us.

The stands were packed with fans cheering as my team, the K-Town Jaguars, was in the lead again with five seconds left in the game. We were playing Mannheim, one of the toughest teams in the league. My teammate passed the ball to me but Mannheim's point guard swatted the ball out of my grasp and ran, undefended, down the court and scored two points, taking the lead. Our coach called the final time out and told us the play.

"Hot Wing!"

## Don't Ask, Don't Tell

We all knew what that meant. Peterson took the ball from the ref and faked a toss to our point guard who was positioned directly behind the defender. Then Peterson lunged the ball toward me down on the right wing in 3 point range. I grabbed the ball in the air, twisted my body and fired the ball into the hoop. One of the Mannheim team members cut my legs from beneath me as I was coming back down. The ball went into the hoop, and my body went into the wood—hard.

"Oooooohhhh shiiiiiittttt!!!!"

That's all I could say. Everything from my left shoulder down to my left ankle was throbbing in pain. I heard a whistle blow and knew that I had a free throw to make because of the foul. The crowd was going crazy! My teammates came and helped me to my feet. In pain, I walked over to the free throw line, hopefully to make the game winning point. As the ball left my hands, I knew that was not going to be the situation. So did my teammates. The ball hit the backboard and our center leaped above everyone else, grabbed the ball and put it back in the hoop for the winning score. Thank goodness cause my shit was nothing but a brick. I limped to the sideline, barely making it before the pain overtook me.

"I got you, babe." I heard Sealyn.

"Suck it up, McPhail got dammit."

Sealyn and Sanders were somewhere in the dizziness around me.

"I got her! Get off, I got her!" Mike was grabbing me out of Sealyn's arms.

"Ouch Mike, shit man. You're making it worse. Let me go!" I groaned.

"She doesn't need your help," he scowled at San and Sealyn. That was all the invitation Sealyn needed.

"You little punk bitch, who the fuck do you think you are? I suggest you stay in ya lane nigga cause you obviously don't know who I am, but I can inform you!" Sealyn pointed at me. "Nigga this is…"

"Sealyn, I'm good. I'm good, y'all!" I pulled myself together enough to stand straight on my own. The pain ebbed in my mental background and their bullshit was in the forefront of my mind. I was so glad this was my last game for the day cause these two were making shit worse.

"I am good," I said again, looking at Mike.

"San, grab my bag please." San grabbed my bag and we started walking to the locker room together.

"So, you're gonna leave with them?" Mike shouted behind us.

I turned around to look at him. He looked at me like he was about to cry or something.

"Mike, I'm going to change my clothes. Can I take a shower and change my clothes? Why are you tripping?" He was getting ridiculous lately.

## Don't Ask, Don't Tell

"He better keep that dumb shit over there where he's at," Sealyn looked dead in his face. Mike started walking toward her and Sealyn slid her hand inside her purse. "You got the right one this time, bitch. Come get some." He stopped in his tracks.

"What the fuck is going on?" I screamed at both of them.

"Mike, I'm going to the locker room. You can't go in there. Please wait out here for me. Sealyn and San come on now. Why are y'all tripping? What's up?

Sealyn stood there in her stilettos like she was about to fucking kill Bill. Then she turned around to walk out of the gym, pausing to say bye. "Bye baby. San, you got her?"

"Yeah, I got her."

Sealyn looked back at Mike again and strut out of the gym like she wished a motherfucker would. I knew there was more to that exchange than met the eye and I was with the right person to get the information.

"San, what the hell was that?"

"Dahni, Sealyn can't stand your boy for some reason and this time I really do not know why. She hates his ass though. That's real talk. I understand why he's jealous. You know how people talk, so he's probably hearing all kinds of bullshit and applying it to y'alls friendship."

"All kinds of bullshit about what?"

"All kinds of bullshit about you fucking with women, nigga, you know what kind of bullshit I'm talking about. So, I'm sure that type of thing weighs on a man and that was where his stupidness was coming from."

"Yes he really has been acting an idiot lately. Its tiring."

"Well, to me, up to this point he's alright. I haven't seen or heard anything foul so far and he is crazy about you. Anybody can see that. Are you happy? That's the real question."

"Yes," I told a half truth. I was just operating inside the guilt that evolved from the knowledge of what my family felt I should be doing— kicking it with a cute guy in a straight relationship. Doing the mainstream thing but I couldn't call that happy. I stayed lit most of the time I was with him and that helped me enjoy myself. It was easier to endure his presence. That's awful to say and think. I just still missed my girl Mimi. I even missed Sealyn these days. But I knew that Mike was who I was really supposed to be with. He would make a good husband.

"Well, if you're happy that's all that matters, Dahni. I'm with you regardless."

"And San, that's exactly why I fucks with you!"

I got dressed and met up with Mike outside the gym. We said bye to San and went over to his room. I went into his fridge and poured myself a shot and a beer.

"DeeDee you drink too much babe."

## Don't Ask, Don't Tell

"That's a great observation, Mike."

"Do you have to drink to be around me? You seem like you're so unhappy sometimes. Like your mind is somewhere else."

Damn. Was it really that obvious?

"You barely touch me, you don't kiss me or show me any affection and you haven't had sex with me since that first time. Don't you want me?"

Here we go.

"I really do care about you Mike. I like our relationship. We're cool."

"But I can tell that you don't love me. I've had girls in love with me before."

"So, you want me to be all over you, Mikey?" I teased.

With an earnest look he said, "I just want it to seem like you want me some kind of way besides me being your homie. I'll do anything for you to just look at me like you look at that bitch in the gym."

I knew he was talking about Sealyn.

"Shit, I wish you would pay me as much attention as you pay to that picture in your room. But you won't even give me the look that you give a picture. I don't know what else to do."

"Will you give me a massage, please?"

# Dahni McPhail

That's what I said to him.

"My body is really, really sore. Please give your girl a massage. Didn't you see that foul I took out there on the court?"

Michael Friday gave me that chip toothed grin and ran into his bathroom to get some lotion so he could give me a massage that he hoped would lead to love making. I threw down a couple more shots and drank my beer and focused my mind on the two things that I knew would get me horny. Mimi and Sealyn.

I took off my clothes and lay naked on his bed. I could see his manhood rise in his shorts. I turned over on my stomach so that he could start massaging my back, where most of my pain from the fall still existed. I heard him kick off his shoes and take off his shirt.

"Where does it hurt, DeeDee?"

"Everywhere, Mikey. You can start with my back."

I was thankful that he took good care of himself. Because of that his hands were nice and smooth enough for me to fool myself into believing they belonged to someone else. He massaged my back with his strong skilled hands and I went to find Mimi in my mind. I felt his hands on my ass and I turned over on my back and spread my legs. He was completely naked. A magnificent specimen of a man with a perfect sized dick. Thick and just the right length. He bent down, taking my nipples in his mouth sucking one, then the other, then both of them at the same time. My nipples hardened and he raised up to look at me. I smiled a smile that satisfied his wondering eyes and pointed at his manhood. He grabbed a magnum and tore it open with his teeth. He was jerking so hard, I reached up and grabbed his tool at the base so it would be still.

"Wait a minute." I got some lube and smothered both of us so it would be a smooth ride. Put the tip at the opening of my pussy and shook all over when he entered me. I gasped at the sheer enormity of the object that was stretching me wide open once again. I had to lift my legs all the way up just for the sake of taking him in comfortably but once I felt his thighs hit the back of my ass, I knew he was in. I bit his lips and sucked his tongue like he liked it while he grinded his hips extracting his dick the entire length and then slowly pushing his thickness back inside me. He thrusted faster and faster and I let him ride me as hard as he wanted. I raised my ass up off the bed in concert with his push and he forcefully pummeled my pussy in return. Then Michael Friday reached around and grabbed my hand, putting my fingers at the crack of his ass. I hoped he didn't see me raise my eyebrow. I guess not. I covered my fingers in the oil that had seeped past his balls down to his ass.

"Here goes nothing," I thought. I slid my middle finger and my forefinger into his ass this time.

"Uuuhnnn!" He winced in pain but he rode my fingers and fucked me like he was about to lose his mind. Two minutes later, it was over. All one hundred and eighty pounds of muscle collapsed on top of me in a breathless heap. He was spent.

Thinking of Mimi and Sealyn helped out a lot with our sex but his reaction to my fingers opened the doors to some nastiness on my part. He liked it and I liked it too. I asked what I wanted to know.

"You like that, Mike? Have you ever done that before?"

"Please don't ever say anything to anyone and no I haven't. You took my virginity. You have to marry me, DeeDee."

"I'm thinking about it a lot, Mike."

"Don't leave me for a girl."

"Don't start. Get up." He rolled over off me onto his back.

"Did you come, DeeDee?" In all this sex, I had never even thought about whether or not I bust a nut.

"Yes, Mike. You made me come three times." I made that shit up. My response worked for him and that was fine with me. I went into his bathroom and cleaned up, then I kissed him and went to my room.

"Hit me later, Dahni."

## Chapter 13

I closed the door behind me and my thoughts went directly to Sealyn. I still wasn't satisfied with what San told me about the problem between her and Mike. Sealyn didn't have a real reason to dislike Mike as much as she did. I wanted to find out what the problem was.

"Nothing, Dahni."

Sealyn didn't want to talk to me about it when I called her. I can't stand when she gets like that.

"Sealyn, I know you're not telling me that you don't have beef with dude, girl. I'm just trying to find out why."

"He doesn't like me because I once dated a girl he was trying to talk to. So him and his dumb ass friends went through the whole calling me a dyke thing and I had to cuss those bitches oooooouuuuuuuuttt!" I laughed as she sang her response to me. "Plus I think he's bi."

"What???!!!!" I heard myself scream.

That is not the type of information that you just drop on somebody, plus I was thinking about his affinity for insertion.

"What, Sealyn? You think he's bi? Are you just saying that shit to piss me off?"

"No. I'm not. I said that's what I 'think.' I didn't say that's what he IS. I only gave you my opinion. He is rather "refined," isn't he?"

My stomach turned inside out at the word "refined." He surely was that.

"Refined, dammit? Refined is your choice of words? Sealyn, do you think this motherfucker is Bi or what? Rather, do you know that this motherfucker is bisexual? "

"I haven't seen the nigga with a dick in his ass if that's what you're asking me, Dahni."

"But you think he's bi?"

"Really, I think I'm just hating, Dahni because he gets to fuck you and I don't. That could be my issue. You know I'm a jealous bitch. On the real, I've never heard or seen that shit."

"And you're a vindictive bitch too."

"But I love you, Dahni nigga. Doubt that never and I'm gonna leave it at that. Is that all you called me for? To talk about him? Don't you want me to come over and make you come?"

## Don't Ask, Don't Tell

Her words caused me to pause. That bitch knew what to do with my pussy.

"No," I croaked. I couldn't cheat on Mimi with her. Damn. I meant I couldn't cheat on Mikey with Sealyn.

"Uh huh. Queen of denial? I love you babe. Bye."

*What I didn't know was on that day was on the other end, after Sealyn hung up the phone with me, she sat there for thirty minutes thinking of how well she actually knew Michael Friday. She knew that he wasn't bi. He was something else completely. That, however, was information that she would not divulge to me until much later in our lives.*

I was learning to like Mike more and more which in turn made the infrequent sex better. We did everything I could think of and it showed in his face that he was all the way in love. I loved him too but he was getting so possessive. He was perfectly fine as long as it was just him and me doing things together. But whenever any of my friends came around, he lost it and was getting worse every day. I didn't give a fuck because I wasn't going to stop hanging with Adrian and Krys and I definitely wasn't going to stop hanging out with San or make Sealyn stop her check ins.

"You can go and hang out with your friends, Mike. You don't have to be around me all the time. I'm not going anywhere. Go somewhere and have some fun with your boys, please."

"OK."

I was shocked. He actually said "yes" and he actually went out. I didn't even want to know where. All I knew was he wasn't going to be at the NCO club tonight while I was DJing and that was a blanket of peace all by itself.

San immediately noticed that Mike was not hovering around.

"Where's your roving guard, Dahni?" San had to get her smart remark in.

"I hope his ass is in another city having some fun and looking at bitches. For real. What's up, San?"

No matter what, San was gonna be at whatever spot I was DJing and she was gonna make sure we had a great time.

"Look, Dahni."

San pointed across the room to this chocolate shorty with thick thighs and a fat ass. She was hot.

"She has been asking me about you for weeks, Dahni. I knew she was gonna be out here tonight."

"Go get her." Nothing wrong with a little conversation, right?

"For real, Dahni? You serious?"

## Don't Ask, Don't Tell

"Yeah, shit. All we're going to do is talk. I just want to see her up close because she is looking like a million bucks from this point of view."

San went over to the other side of the club and brought "Devita" over to the DJ's booth. She was as cute up close as she was from a distance with those dimples.

I chatted with her for a few minutes and exchanged phone numbers.

"Are you really gonna call me?" she inquired.

I'm a good friend. I always call.

"Friend? Yeah, right? I want you. Real talk dot com, DJ." She laughed and walked away.

It seemed like more girls wanted me since I was unavailable to them but even though I still had desires, I was chilling with Mike and every day I was starting to see him as my husband and the father of my children. His jealousy would pass once we were married.

The rest of the night went great and when it was over, I felt like a champ walking from the club on my way back to my dorm. It was a nice, cool summer night and I was gonna chill and wake up and take Mikey to get some breakfast in the morning.

"So who was that girl you were talking to?" I'll be damned, this stealth ass nigga.

"Damnit, Michael Friday! You scared the shit out of me!"

Where the hell did this man come from? He wrapped his arms around me and pulled me to him as we walked together.

"I'm sorry, DeeDee. I didn't mean to scare you. You didn't answer any of my texts back."

"I thought this was our night off, Mike. I thought we were doing down time, " I sighed.

"Completely off? No texts or nothing, Dahni? Where do people in relationships do that at?"

"Hereville," I quipped.

"I'm staying with you tonight," he stated adamantly.

Now, if he hadn't stalked up on me, I might have gone into my room and called him so he could come over and get some pussy. But now, I was exasperated. We had to fix this crazy shit starting tomorrow.

"You're telling me you're staying with me Mike?"

"No, I'm asking, Dahni," he said, changing his tone and grinning. "Can I stay with you?"

"You can walk me to my room, Mike."

### Don't Ask, Don't Tell

"Oh, cause you got that dyke bitch coming over to your fucking room, so I can't come over?"

"Oh my gosh, Mike, why are you tripping? I'm not meeting anyone in my room. Go home. Just go to your room please. Take a chill pill, tonight." I pulled away from him and started jogging.

"You don't want to fuck me because you want to fuck bitches! I know you're still fucking bitches, Dahni."

I stopped in my tracks and turned around so I could see his face. His voice sounded so strange, I had to look. I wanted to see if his face matched what I heard. When I looked at him, he forced a smile.

"You barely want to make love with me but you're always smiling in some bitches face, DeeDee."

"What bitch, Mike? What bitches? You're so fucking insecure. Go head somewhere with that dumb shit, man. Take your ass home. Fuck you with that bull shit you bitch ass nigga." I started jogging to my room again.

Mike tread the distance between us in what seemed like a millisecond. By this time I was standing at the corner from my dorm and he had come up the hill and caught up with me. Fast.

"The bitch you were talking to in the club tonight, Dahni! That's what bitch! I saw you!!!"

This nigga was screaming so loud at me, I thought everybody in the quad would wake up and look out of their window. And there was that look I remembered from my room.

"So you were stalking me at the club, Mike?" I looked him dead in his eyes. He seemed to snap out of his trance realizing what he said.

"Yes, I stopped by and saw you."

"So you saw that I'm not talking to any girls then, Mike. I'm only dating you! I'm a DJ. I get plenty of numbers every time I DJ. They are numbers for future gigs. I have to network, Mike. Can you calm down, please"

I was trying to talk this nigga down because I really hadn't seen this side of him before, nor did I expect this tonight. He was straight trippin.

"Look, I'm about to go into my room and lay it down for the night. I'll talk to you tomorrow, OK? First thing in the morning. I can't do this tonite, Mike." I stretched my arms out so he could come and give me a hug and a kiss.

He seemed to chill. "OK, DeeDee. I'm sorry. I just don't want to keep hearing these motherfuckers telling me I told you so and that once a dyke always a dyke shit.'

"Stop listening to people and deal with what you see with me. Deal with me, what you see with us and not what you hear from these fuckin' haters. That's your main problem. I'm going upstairs."

## Don't Ask, Don't Tell

I just did not have the energy to debate my sexuality on top of the rest of his antics tonight. He'd already scared the shit completely out of me. I was just ready to go to bed. As I walked to the door of my building, a car horn beeped at me. I turned around and it was Devita and some friends. I guessed they were going home. I waved at them then went inside to my room. I took a shower and lay down in my bed. I don't think I had been sleep for an hour when I felt his weight on top of me.

"So, you think I didn't see that bitch leaving, DeeDee? Huh? You fucking dyke?

"Oh my God, Mike! How did you get in my room?" Michael was naked and bearing down on me with all of his weight.

"Remember I'm the logistics officer. I control the keys for all the buildings in our organization, BITCH!"

For some reason, I was not as afraid as maybe I should have been. I guess I thought I could talk him down. Right then and there would have been the perfect time to scream for my life. I should have been more afraid given the strong stench of liquor all over him and that crazed look in his eyes.

"OK, Mikey. OK baby. You're here now. Lay down next to me."

"Lay down and do what? Go to sleep, dyke. You led me on all this fucking time pretending that you like me when all you want to do is be with a woman. I saw that black bitch leaving!"

I flashed back to the horn blowing at me as Devita and her friends drove off.

"Mikey, I wasn't with anyone tonight. I came in here, took my shower and…"

"Shut up! Shut up, dyke before I kill you right now!"

His grey eyes pierced the darkness. He straddled me, clasping my throat with his beautiful hands. I felt tears from his eyes splashing on my face. Fear then seized me.

"Mikey, you're hurting me. Please, I promise you I was not with anyone tonight. No one was in my room."

"Shut up you fucking lying dyke! You want to be a man? Huh? You want to be a man fucking me in my ass bitch!"

His whisper sounded like a shriek in the darkness. Tears rained from his eyes all over my face and neck. His grip tightened around my neck. I tried to scream for help but it was too late for that. Nothing would come out. I couldn't make a sound. I kicked and scratched his arms as he pried my legs apart and ripped into me with and angry thrust. A muffled sound stuck in my throat as I felt the unbearable pain. He punched me in the face over and over and I faded.

I woke up when I felt his iron tear into me from behind. It was pitch black and hard to breathe. I realized he had my face smashed into my pillow as he tore my anal cavity open.

## Don't Ask, Don't Tell

"Yeah bitch. You gonna get all this dick in your ass now. You like this shit you fucking dyke. I hate you!" Tears dropped from his eyes onto the back of my head and my back. With every single word he slammed into my rectum harder and harder. Over and over. I cried out in pain and felt his hands squeezing my neck from behind. Blackness took me away again.

I could barely breathe when my eyes opened again. I couldn't cry. I couldn't believe he was still raping me. All I could do was moan. My own tears rolled down my face onto my bed as his hugeness continued to tear into me. I resigned myself to the fact that he was going to kill me when he was done. Maybe before.

"You bitch. You never wanted to fuck me. Not even once!" he wailed as he slammed into me as hard as he could.

I managed to squeeze out a "Please" between his fingers. It only enraged him further. He beat my lips.

"Shut up! Shut up!" It was so strange that he whispered in this shrieking voice the entire time. He grabbed my throat again and squeezed hard, blocking any oxygen I might have gotten, still battering my insides endlessly. Thankfully, I blacked out again.

The next time I opened my eyes, it was morning and I was alone. I raised up only to feel pain searing through every entrance in my entire body.

Michael had literally raped me all night. I don't know how many times. I thought he was going to kill me for sure. I pulled myself out of the bed and found that I had bled everywhere. I went into the bathroom to take a shower and was shocked to see my face. Both my eyes were black, my mouth split and swollen and a set of clearly defined, red hand print bruises colored my neck. He ejaculated all over me from my hair to my feet.

"Damn. I gotta call San." That's all I could think.

Before I could get over to my cell phone, San was banging and screaming at me from outside, not knowing what lay behind my door.

"Dahni, get your ass up man. You know we're supposed to be going to Frankfurt this morning."

I struggled from the bathroom to the door, using the walls to hold me up as I went. When I opened the door, San's face confirmed my condition. As soon as she saw me, she turned fiery red. I fell into her arms.

"What the fuck happened, Dahni? Who did this to you?!!!"

"Mike," I could barely speak. My throat felt like I had rocks in it.

"That motherfucker did this shit, Dahni! Imma kill that bitch! I'mma kill that motherfuckin bitch, Dahni! Oh my God baby, look what he did to you!"

### Don't Ask, Don't Tell

San's voice reached a high pitched scream. I motioned to her to be quiet so that she would not draw attention from the building watch officer.

Then I told her about my night.

"He raped you, Dahni? Look at you! He did all this shit to you? That motherfucker. Imma kill him. God I'mma kill that bitch!" Her voice broke as the words came from her throat. I knew she was gonna cry. "We have to get you to the hospital."

"No. We can't." I found my voice. "He's gonna get put out of the Army."

San's face reflected a murderous intent. She could barely contain herself, "so the fuck what! I don't give a fuck what happens to his has, Dahnil. Look what he did to you!"

"San, it's my fault. I shouldn't have talked to him in the first place. I knew I didn't love him like he loved me. He wasn't like this at first. He snapped last night because he thought Devita was in my room. He just lost it."

San was not listening to me. She was on the phone.

"Get over here now, Sealyn. Hurry up!"

"No. Don't tell Sealyn, man." It was too late.

## Dahni McPhail

San walked around the room looking like a detective. "He thought who was in your room? What? How the fuck did he get in here anyway? Did you leave the door open?

"Nah, San. I locked it. He said he been made a key because he knew I was still fucking women but I wasn't, San. You know I wasn't. You should have seen his face, San. I swear I was looking at the devil."

Thinking about that face made me shiver with fear. "He looked like a monster, San." Pictures from last night flooded my head as I sat on the edge of my bed. Tears rolled down my face.

"You should have seen his eyes, San, you should have seen them."

"Boom, boom, boom! Boom, boom, boom!

"Dahni! San! Open the door!"

If all hell hadn't broken loose yet, I knew it was about to. Sealyn was at the door. San got up and let her in.

"Look what that sorry motherfucker did to her, Sealyn."

San was sobbing openly now. My back was to the door as I sat on the bed still covered in semen and blood. Sealyn walked around to my front and I looked up at her. I swear on my life, right then I saw the same monster in her eyes then that I saw last night. I saw death. Sealyn's hazel eyes turned black right in front of my face and her skin paled. When she spoke, however, she was surprisingly calm.

## Don't Ask, Don't Tell

"Did Friday do this to you?" Her voice was laced with steel. When I didn't answer, she asked again with the same tone.

"Did Friday do this to you, Dahni?"

"Yes, Sealyn, but I don't want to report it."

"What did he do to you, baby?"

I retold the horrible story as much as I could remember.

"I don't want to relive this thing over and over, Sealyn. I just need to recover."

"OK, you don't have to report it. Come on. Let's get you in the shower."

San leaped across the room screaming, "You're a motherfuckin lie! We're reporting this shit! This motherfucker is gonna pay for this shit with his career!"

Sealyn, who was strangely calm even after hearing everything I said, looked at San squarely in the eyes.

"She doesn't want to report it. That's it and that's that. She's not going to report it, I'm not going to report it and you're not going to report it. San, you're gonna take care of Dahni."

"Bullshit, bitch. You're crazy." San started for the door and Sealyn grabbed San back with a strength I did not know she had. She shocked Sanders into silence.

"Sanders, this is what's gonna happen. Dahni needs to request leave and you're gonna take her home with you until she recovers. We're not going to report it and we're not going to tell anyone else about this. Ever. Do you understand me?"

Sealyn Scott sounded like the devil. He voice was as cold as ice. She still had San by the arm damn near off her feet. "Do you understand that this stays between us forever, Sanders?

San couldn't say a word. I think she was in shock. Sealyn returned her attention to me. "Come on, baby. Let's go into the shower so I can check you out."

Sealyn was an RN before she came into the military to get away from her "girlfriend." She cleaned me up with gentle, loving care and dressed my wounds.

"He raped you anally too, Dahni?" she asked. She checked me thoroughly.

I dropped my eyes to the floor as the tears burned my face again. I couldn't say the word "rape" again. Sealyn kissed my cheek.

"Its OK, baby. You don't need stitches. You're gonna be OK and we're gonna do what you want to do. Can I ask you something?"

## Don't Ask, Don't Tell

I looked at Sealyn.

"Do you think you want an apology from him?"

That was really strangest of questions.

"An apology?" I was blown away by the question. "No. I'll be fine. I just don't want to ever see him again as long as I live. I just want him to go away, far away, and leave me alone. Nothing more, nothing less."

"Well, if you aren't going to report him to the Military Police, I am!"

Sanders was snapped back into the situation, still not trying to hear what I was saying or what Sealyn was saying.

"If he doesn't get reported, I'm going to have to kill him, Sealyn. I can't live knowing that he's done this to Dahni. I can't let him live. He will pay for this one way or another."

Sealyn walked over and put her arms around San and hugged her.

"San, we're going to do this the way Dahni wants it done. Let's respect her wishes. I'm gonna go and talk to a friend of mine so we can get Friday on some orders back to the States immediately. He will be gone in a week. Let's do this like Dahni wants it done."

"How is Dahni gonna handle this if nothing happens to him? She's gonna need therapy. She's gonna be living in fear."

"No I'm not, San. I'm gonna be fine. I just need my regular face back and some time off to heal. I'm cool. I'll get some counseling. Just don't tell anyone, please. No one, San. I'm swearing you to secrecy. Both of you!! Promise me to God."

"That's bullshit, Dahni!"

"Promise me, San. Promise me to God that you will not tell anyone including Adrian, Krys or Mimi. No one. Please. No one." I started crying again.

"Promise Dahni that you will never tell, Sanders." Sealyn co-signed my pact. "Dahni is going to make it through this. We'll see her through it. Friday's going back to the states, and she can move on with her life and forget all about this."

Today, for once in her life, Sealyn was not full of drama. She was methodical in her actions. Along with my tears, she secured San's word. Then, she fixed my body, sent me home with San for three weeks and by the time I got back, Michael Friday was gone to Fort Polk, Louisiana. Gone from my life for good. Forever.

My stay with San brought me back to life. She took great care of me and by the time my leave was up, my body and face were back to normal. My physical scars were nearly gone and my mental scars were following closely behind. I've never been one to dwell in the past because I feel there is nothing I can change in yesterday. I was moving on.

## Don't Ask, Don't Tell

I was back in my room watching a movie when my phone rang. "Dahni, how was your leave? Did you bring us back anything?" It was my boys Krys and Adrian.

"Hell no! What's up?"

"You wanna run with us up to Frankfurt right quick? We're picking up the turn tables from the shop." I missed Krys and Adrian so much. More than they could ever know. "We'll be back before ten."

"Aiite. I'm with it." Normalcy. I grabbed my jacket and headed out the door to meet up with them. "Damn!" I was almost down the stairs when I realized that my ID card wasn't in my jacket. I couldn't leave the post without it.

I started looking everywhere for my ID card, but couldn't find it. Then, I spotted my gym bag and looked in it. No dice. I unzipped the side pocket and there it was. I reached inside to get it and felt something else. Some paper. I pulled out the paper and looked at it. It was a note on a torn piece of paper. I reached in my gym bag pocket and got the other half. I opened it and put it together. This was Sealyn's handwriting. Damn. I had forgotten all about the letter Sealyn left at the hotel that morning over a year ago. I read it and it made my heart fill with love for her.

> *"Dahni, I know it's hard for you to deal with what you are feeling right now. That's why I thought it was best for me not to be here when you awakened. I didn't want to be here if you were going through your guilt thing and tripping.*

*Plus, I have some business to take care of. I want to be with you. I am willing to do whatever it takes... including dealing with my lover. I will leave her if I can be with you. That's how much I love you. I didn't tell you because I didn't want to stress you out, but Drill Sergeant Jones is the X I was telling you about. She got her friends to send me to basic training where she works and she won't let me go. But I will go AWOL, call the police on her, or report her. I will do whatever it takes if you will just tell me that you love me as much as I love you. I will give up everything for you Dahni. I live for you. I'm willing to fight with her for you and surely, I will die for you. I will do anything for you. Please call me and tell me that you want to be with me too. I will be at my mother's for a week...*

Damn. I dropped the letter to the floor and fell to my knees with it. All this time, I've hated Sealyn and thought she was lying to me about loving me but she really was ride or die. She was "in" love with me all that time. She was literally going to risk her life to be with me and my ignorance and stupidity shoved her right back into the arms of her abusive lover. Wow. And she loved me enough to take second place behind Mimi but still see me through the worst time of my life. Damn! I was sick.

My phone rang again. "We're outside in front."

"Alright." I flushed the letter and went outside to meet my up with Adrian and Krys.

"Dee, who pissed in your corn flakes?"

"Let's get some drinks, man," I said. "I need a fucking drink."

## Don't Ask, Don't Tell

For a few minutes, I thought my life's recent events were going to overwhelm me. Sealyn had been so faithful and loyal to me. She'd loved me all the time. "Let's get some Patron, y'all."

"Not a problem." My friends were always down for a shot.

We got on the autobahn and headed to Frankfurt. "Push this shit, Adrian!" Krys was telling Adrian to speed up. There was no speed limit on the autobahn and we always went as fast as the car would take us.

"Dahni, look." Adrian was telling me to look at the speedometer. I realized that he was looking at it too and not at the highway.

Then Krys screamed, "Oh shit!" A truck had stalled in the middle of the autobahn and we were headed directly for it! Adrian swerved to the right to miss it. He hit the brakes but the car just wouldn't stop. It slid off the autobahn. That's all I remember.

**Dahni McPhail**

## Chapter 14

I woke up in the hospital looking at two familiar faces. Adrian and Krys. They both had bandages on their heads, but at least they were OK. "What happened, Krys?"

"Two drunk ass idiots were stopped in the road and damn near killed us. We slid off the autobahn and the back end of our car hit a tree. It just messed up the trunk but you hit your head and your leg was caught in the back. Other than that, we're all OK."

Why did I feel so sick, then?

"I have to go get the nurse for you, Dahni. I'll be right back." Krys walked out the door to go and get the attending.

"Adrian, are we in trouble?" I remembered we had been drinking.

"Nope. It wasn't our fault and they didn't blow us."

"Good! Life is grand!" That would have been all we needed! I was outwardly celebrating with them but inwardly I was thinking to myself, "what else could possibly happen to me?"

Krys walked back in with the nurse and she made them leave so that she could talk to me.

"Frau McPhail, I'm sorry to tell you. You lost the baby."
"Huh?"

"You had a miscarriage…"

The rest of the conversation with her telling me that I was going to be fine and I could leave the hospital in the morning ebbed in the background. All I kept hearing was "miscarriage."

"Miscarriage. I was pregnant by Michael and didn't know it. Damn, and I lost my baby.

"You'll be discharged tomorrow morning and you just need to follow up with your primary care provider in three weeks. Frau McPhail, you and your friends were very lucky today. You should be more careful. You may not be this lucky again!"

Miscarriage. The nurse left and I was laying there, still in a daze when Mianya rushed into the room.

Trish, and Diana were right behind her. "Dahni! Dahni, are you OK? Trish and Diana's faces were panic-stricken. Mianya stopped mid step when she saw me.

"Yeah, I'm fine." The second the word "fine" came out of my mouth, Mianya rushed over to me and started bawling uncontrollably. Here she was after all these months.

"D, we're going to go and see if we can get out of this hospital tonight. We'll be back." Adrian and Krys left the room.

"Dahni, what were you guys thinking? What is wrong with you! You could have been killed!" Mianya was crying but somehow still managed to give me a lecture.

I was about to say, "How about we start at this point: I haven't seen your ass in six months and the last time I did see you, you were kissing a bitch in the park." I didn't say it though because I was more glad to see that woman than anyone or anything I'd seen lately.

"Mimi, I'm OK. I sprained my leg or something and got knocked out. That's all."

"What happened to your face?" She pointed at one of the scars from the Friday incident.

"Basketball," I lied.

Trish got on her rant, "Um, first of all we haven't heard hide nor hair from your ass in forever, then the next thing we hear is that your ass is in a car accident and damn near dead. You're going to have to stop hanging out, balling, or riding or whatever you're doing with your silly ass male friends, Dahni. They clocked the car at doing over 150 mph before it crashed. The car you guys were in is totaled!"

Damn. Trish and Di both were on my ass, now. Women get a whole lot more excited than guys about shit like this 'cause her description of the car being totaled was different than Adrian's "dented trunk" discription. I knew the accident wasn't that bad. It couldn't be, given the fact that we'd gone much faster than that many times before.

"Ain't I in the hospital? Can I be injured without a lecture?"

Even though I was talking shit I knew Trish was right about the judgment call. Mianya was still lying next to me holding me. I started to feel so safe again.

Adrian and Krys came back with their good news. They were headed home. "I'm going to stay with her," Mianya said. Then she asked Trish and Diana to get some things and bring them back for her and for me. They both gave me hugs and kisses before leaving and told me they would be back in the morning to get me and take me to their place so I could recover. Mianya finally stopped crying and sat next to my bed in the chair.

"Heeeeyyy, Mimi. Hey, cutie." Mianya looked at me and started crying again. "Girl, stop crying. I'm alright."

"I know. I know you're all right. I was just so scared. You remember the last time I saw you. I didn't know what to think or how to act. Then Adrian called Trish to tell her what happened and asked her to find me. When Trish told me, I just fell apart. We've been so far apart and I thought you were dead or dying"

I was thinking to myself, "Wow my dawg Adrian called Trish to find Mimi so she could come and get me. That's my friend."

"I'm sorry I moved out and I haven't talked to you. I'm sorry, for all this time apart and these other people in our lives. I don't care about any of it. I just want to start from right here. I realized today that if something happened to you, I wouldn't have been able to forgive myself." She came over, got in the bed and lay next to me again. I wrapped my arms around her and held her. Mianya was crying from the depths of her heart.

"I just want to start here, Dahni." I guess this wasn't the time to tell her about anything. Would there ever be a time? One thing was for sure. I would have been a fool to not realize and understand that this woman truly cared about me. I chose to remain silent and I just held her.

Morning came. Trish and Diana showed up bright and early to pick us up and take me to their apartment. My leg was not broken, but I was on crutches and had some serious pain pills. Pain pills, Patron and beer is what I was thinking would bring immediate relief of pain and memories.

We arrived at the apartment. Not long after we got there, the doorbell started ringing and kept ringing. Everyone came over to see how I had been and how was doing. I was propped up on the couch and Mimi was tending to my every want and need. The doorbell rang and Adrian and Krys walked in. Now I knew I was busted with the girl on girl business.

"Hey everybody." Adrian and Krys spoke as they came inside. All the ladies were still coupled up and chilling with their girlfriends. Krys and Adrian acted like nothing was going on. "Dahni, you want to take a shot?" *My friends were thinking exactly like me.* "It'll make your pills work better."

"You know it, Krys. Pour it." I was ready to take a hit.

Mianya snapped! "Haven't these two hooligans talked you into enough crazy shit, Dahni? Adrian and Krys, Dahni is not drinking with her medication!"

Krys and Adrian backed back. "Alright Mianya"

"Aiite." Hmmm… I know I never told Krys and Adrian about the lesbian side but these two were OK with everything that was going on around them? They were the ones who called *Trish* to find *Mianya*. I didn't even know they knew them. Damn. Do my friends already think I'm like that?

"You two shouldn't be drinking either. Do you remember you were just in an accident, crazies?" Mimi admonished my friends.

"Yeah, but we're drinking trying to forget our pain!" They laughed and everybody else in the house laughed. "Dahni, we just came over to make sure you were good. We still have to DJ tonight. Mianya, you got her?"

"You know I do. Thank you guys so much. Thank you for finding me." Mianya gave Adrian a hug. Then Mianya gave Krys a hug. They hugged Trish and Diana and they went out of the door. Right.

I was blown away by the fact that my boys were so cool with everything and...Well, I just didn't get it. I had no idea they even knew all these people and, hugs? Hugs? I was blown. I guess Mianya felt the need to respond to the look that was on my face. I know I was still shell shocked from Mike's rantings about lesbians and that experience exacerbated my own uncertainties.

"Dahni, your friends are very nice guys in spite of their mental illness. They love you, they are cool with you, and they really don't care about your personal life. You don't have to be shocked at their comfort level. This is nothing new to them. They are not surprised or appalled. Sweetie, everybody knows that you're a lesbian—except for you. OK?"

# Dahni McPhail

*

Mimi had no idea what she just said to me but that small speech answered thousands of questions. I heard Mike's voice, "Once a dyke, always a dyke."

The week went by pretty fast. I was up and walking around a couple of days after I was released from the hospital. It touched my heart that the ladies from the parties stopped by to see me and make sure I was OK. They'd been thinking about me all this time. I guess that's where the word "family" came from. They really treated me like I was a little sister or something. Mianya was there for everything. From physical therapy to making sure my friends didn't coerce me into drinking and taking pills at the same time. By Friday, I was ready to hit the streets.

"Mimi lets go to dinner."

"Where do you want to go baby?" "Baby" sounded so good when she said it.

One of the things I'd grown to love about Germany was the food. The basic meal content and preparation was so different than what I was used to in the states. There was a nice family owned diner down the street from Trish and Di's and that's where we went.

Mianya and I walked to the spot on the corner and sat down for a nice meal. I ordered my favorite, Sauerbraten, which is beef marinated in vinegar and spices then oven roasted. I got a double side of Spatlze or homemade noodles. Mimi ordered the Chicken Schnitzel with gypsy gravy and Spatzle. We both started with Gurken Salat or pickled salad. Awesome food. Then we asked for a couple of Hefferweizen with a shot of Ouzo on the side. When our drinks arrived, I took my shot and looked at Mimi earnestly.

"Mianya, how do lesbian relationships work?" She laughed.

"What?" Why was she laughing at me?

"Dahni, they work just like any other relationship. It's just that there are two women together. They have the same issues and difficulties. There is nothing different. I mean, sometimes you run into people who say dumb stuff when they see you together or your family might not accept it. Other than that, it's the same as any other relationship. Why?"

"I was just wondering. My friends and I used to think it was something that you did to not get pregnant and have fun until you met the man you were going to marry." She laughed again.

"Well, some people are like that. They are considered bi-sexual or just doing what they do. They dibble and dabble but mainly stay in a relationship with a man. A lesbian has a sexual preference for women. They like and are sexually attracted to women. Men don't do anything for them." I thought about myself and my struggles with orgasms in my previous relationship with Friday.

"Most lesbians are like that from birth. Something or someone always happens to make them come to terms with how they feel and what they want. There are some, though, who never come to terms with who they are." Again, my relationship with Michael ran through my mind. I thought about how much I tried to love him and how I made myself look forward to a life with him. I tried so hard to love him, to enjoy him and be in love with him.

"Everybody deals with their sexuality in their own due time, Dahni. Can I ask you something?" Oh, shit.

"Sure."

"Were you in love with that guy?"

\*

We left the restaurant and headed back to Trish's and Diana's. We walked very slowly. Mimi put my arm around her shoulder and put her arm around my waist. I felt so comfortable with her. She was such a good friend. We were talking and laughing as we came into the apartment. All the laughing stopped when we saw Sealyn. She was sitting at the table with a black eye and a busted lip. Mimi ran to Sealyn and put her arms around her.

"Oh my God, Sealyn! Don't tell me that moron jumped on you again!" Sealyn started crying. The only thing I could think of was that motherfuckin TJ put her hands on Sealyn again and this time my rage was at a totally different level. Trish headed out the door. "I'm going over there," she said.

"Me too." I was going to kick TJ's ass no later than that very night. Sealyn screamed.

"No, Dahni! You can't go. You can't! You're the reason why she hit me!"

Everybody in the house took a pause. Mianya backed up and said, "What?"

"When I heard that you were in an accident Dahni, I wanted to come and see you but she wouldn't let me. She's been mad at me all week. She started drinking early this morning. Then, tonight I asked her did she want to get out of the house and come to see Trish and Diana. I didn't even know you were still here. T slapped me and told me that she would kill you and me if she found out that we were sleeping together again! She started hitting me but I was able to push her down. She was so drunk she couldn't get up. I ran out the house, took the car and came here!

Well. Yet another cat was let out of a bag. Sealyn was back to her dramatic antics. I understood how Sealyn was hurting and all but, damn. Did she have to say what she said about us sleeping together? *A-fucking-gain?* Mianya hugged Sealyn like she hadn't heard a word. "It's OK, Sealyn. You're safe now. She won't come in here."

"I'm going over there to check on T and to talk to her. This shit has to cease." Trish started out the door again. I followed her. Trish turned around and said, "I got this Dahni. We don't need for a bad situation to get worse."

Diana and Mianya comforted and cared for Sealyn. Mianya still didn't treat her differently even after hearing about the reason for Sealyn's fight. That's Mianya. I went in the fridge, got a beer and sat on the couch fuming. They put Sealyn in the additional bedroom and Diana stayed in there with her so she could fall asleep. Mianya came down into the front room with me.

She sat down on the couch and laid her head on my lap. Then she looked up at me. "I don't know why she stays, baby."

"She's afraid, Mimi. She's afraid to get hurt if she leaves. That's why somebody needs to kick Jones' ass one good time so she can see what it feels like to get fucked up. Trust me. That's all it'll take to cut that shit short."

Mianya put her arm around me. "Something is wrong with T, Dahni. When she drinks, all she wants to do is fight. She's just not like that when she is sober. I mean, she is always silly-crazy but not crazy-crazy."

"Well she needs to get fucked up, fucked up." I said. Inwardly I wanted to fuck somebody up anyway.

After about three hours, the door opened and Trish walked in. Diana came down from Sealyn's room. "Well, baby?"

"T was crying, sorry, you know the routine. She said she'll never do it again." Mianya jumped up.

"Oh my God, she always says that! That's a crock of shit!" Trish looked at Mimi and Diana.

"I know. But tonight I made her ass go and get some help. I took her to the rehab center on post and made her turn herself in and I'm gonna make sure she stays in there until she gets her shit together. I mean that. Enough is enough!" Mianya applauded Trish's announcement.

"Thank you, Jesus!"

*

"Is Sealyn sleep, Di?" Trish asked.

"Yeah, baby." Diana walked over and put her arms around Trish.

"Alright. Let her rest until the morning. Dahni, Mimi, we're going to bed. I think this has been enough excitement for the week, month and year." And a lifetime, I thought.

"Good night, y'all."

Mianya looked at me. "I'm going to turn in, Dahni."

"K." We went up to her room. By the time I got in the bed, Mianya was already lying there looking at the ceiling.

"What's up, Mimi?" I turned off the light and pulled her close to me.

"You smell good," she said.

"Thanks. What are you thinking about, Mimi?"

"You."

"Me? I'm right here."

"I mean just everything about you, Dahni. Something is different about you. Something is heavy on your mind." I knew this conversation was coming.

"Mysterious me. What is it that you want to know, Mianya?"

"Are you going to be honest?"

"Yeah. As honest as I can be."

"What's really going on or has gone on with you and Sealyn?" Shit, I can answer that.

"Nothing is going on. But we do have history. . ." I gave Mimi a very brief and detail lacking rundown on the Dahni and Sealyn saga with emphasis on the fact that it was all over.

## Don't Ask, Don't Tell

"Thank you for being honest, Dahni."

"Mianya, I'll always try to be honest with you. You just don't go tripping and changing on Sealyn now that you know we have history. There's nothing to us anymore."

"I can handle mine. You just handle yours, McPhail."

"Mimi, wanna know what I've been thinking about?"

"What, Dahni?"

"Well, I've been thinking about you, Miss Mianya. Thinking about how good you've been to me and how well you've taken care of me. I really appreciate you. Thank you so much. You're a really good friend." She turned to me.

"Is that all I am, Dahni? A really good friend?"

I could feel her breath on my lips. "Dahni, are you telling me that all I am is a really good friend to you? Do you feel me?" I wanted to say everything but nothing came out. Instead, I took her face into my hands and kissed her. The kiss had been a long time coming. I kissed her with all the love I'd been lying about feeling for women for so very long. I kissed her for what seemed like forever. Mianya pulled her lips from mine, then wrapped her arms around me and hugged me as tight as she could. "Dahni, I love you so much."

I wasn't finished. I gently put her on her back and began kissing her again. I moved my body on top of hers. I took my leg and spread her legs open so she could feel me against her completely. My hips were in motion. "Dahni. . ." I silenced her with a passionate kiss. My tongue entered her warm, soft mouth. Her tongue was enthusiastically masturbating mine; my tongue was masturbating hers. I plunged my tongue deep into her mouth repeatedly then seized her tongue, sucking it with just enough pressure. She moaned. Chills went through my body. I knew it was time to make love to Mianya.

My lips eagerly went after her ear as I attempted to taste and enjoy every part of her. I covered her neck with hot moist kisses. Her body writhed beneath mine. I could feel the heat between her legs. She opened her legs wider and pushed herself against me. I responded to her thrusts with a thrust of my own. When my body met her body, she grabbed my ass and pulled me even closer to her. She started rocking her clit against me. Then she wrapped her legs around mine. I didn't want to take my lips off her for one second, but I did so I could take off my wife beater and my boxers. Then I removed Mimi's clothes. She was completely naked. Her beautiful, brown skin was flawless with chocolate perky nipples that stood at attention. I knew they were waiting for me to suck them. I took her nipples into my mouth. Mimi moaned with pleasure. "Dahni, come on. Please…" I knew what she wanted. I could feel her wetness. She opened her legs and her clit rested warmly on my thigh while I continued devouring her breasts. She grabbed me again and started thrusting feverishly. She wanted to come. I let her do that for a minute. Then, I worked my way down her body, getting more and more excited with every kiss. I loved Mianya and I wanted her so much.

Mianya moaned loudly as I slid my fiery tongue between her lips. "Daaahhhhnniii." Her voice was sexy, so beautiful. She was so horny and so wet. My tongue and lips glided over every part of her wetness. Mianya's body was going crazy. It made me get even wilder. I lifted her up by her buttocks and buried my face in her excitement, plunging my tongue deeply. "Aaaaaaaaaaahhh! Ooooohhhh, Dahni, please baby!" My tongue went inside her exploring her warmth, tasting and tantalizing her as she writhed against me. As I continued making love to her with my long, blazing tool, I felt her thighs start closing in on me. I knew she was close to an orgasm but I didn't want her to come yet. I wanted my fingers inside when she came. I backed off long enough to slide my fingers inside her to the hilt. I wanted to do more, but Mianya exploded as soon as I entered her.

Then she kept coming. She grabbed me and pulled me up to meet her lips. She kissed me and kept moving her body against my hand. So, I kept making love to her. It only lasted a minute. She locked her lips on my shoulder; her body was gyrating frantically to my lovemaking. She tried to keep her lips against my shoulder I guess to muffle the sounds, but she was loud as fuck. "Dahni, I love you. I love you." I could feel the wetness of her love running all over my hand. She scratched me, bit me, and I was wearing it out. She gave it all to me. She screamed and I felt a quick stream of heated joy spray my hand as she came again.

I held her as her breathing slowed. She lay beneath me with her legs and arms still wrapped around me. I rested my weight on my arms and waited for her to say something. She turned toward me and kissed me. It was a nice, soft kiss. The kiss of two people who loved each other, regardless of gender.

I gave her another kiss and rolled off her onto my back. Mimi followed me, kissing me. She pushed her hair out of the way and said, "I want to make you feel like you made me feel." She took her leg and spread mine, then began to put her hand down into my wetness. I really don't know what happened but I just freaked. I felt like someone threw hot lava on me and then a bucket of ice water right behind it. I trembled uncontrollably. I grabbed her hands when I heard someone screaming and crying in the background. Then, I realized it was me!

"Dahni, what's wrong?!!!! Baby, what's wrong? What's going on??!!!"

Mimi was on her feet with me.

"What's wrong, baby? I'm sorry! I'm sorry, Dahni!" She grabbed me and held me tight. My body was stiff as a board.

"Tell me what's wrong, Dahni. Baby I'll do anything to help you, just tell me. Please tell me."

"Mimi, I don't want that. I don't want to! Please stop. Please don't hurt me!"

## Don't Ask, Don't Tell

"What do you mean, Dahni? I would never hurt you. OK. We don't have to, baby. We don't have to. Please tell me what's wrong, Dahni! Please!"

Could I tell her that recently I was raped mercilessly? Could I tell her that just a few days ago, I found out I'd lost a baby I didn't know that I was pregnant with? My rapists' baby? I'd tried to push it all to the back of my mind. That night, I laid on that bed and cried myself to sleep in Mimi's arms.

I was so glad that Mimi was Mimi. She stopped asking questions and just held me until I went to sleep. Somehow that was everything I needed.

## Chapter 15

By the time we all got up and went downstairs in the morning, Sealyn was gone.

"I knew she wasn't going to be here."

Diana went straight to the phone and started dialing. She got off the phone and announced to us that Sealyn was at home and she was OK. I think we all breathed a sigh of relief. Not Trish though.

"Was T there?"

"She didn't say, baby." Trish got on the phone. I sat on the couch. This was too much drama for me. Not the fact that Sealyn went home. I can understand not wanting to be around anyone. I'm talking about possibly going and picking up TJ's crazy ass and then going home. That, I could not understand. Mianya came and sat next to me and put her arms around me. I know she was still thinking about last night. I also knew that she wasn't going to say another word about it until I was ready to have the conversation.

"What time do you want to go back to the room?" she asked.

I looked at her. I must have looked at her like I thought she was sending me away because she said, "I'm coming with you, I just wanted to know baby." I smiled. I was relieved that she could feel my concern without me having to say it.

"I have to do a couple of things at home. I'm studying for the sergeant's board now."

"OK. Let's catch the bus and go then. It's not going to take long." We went upstairs and got our things.

Trish asked, "You guys leaving? I'll give you a ride. You don't have to take the bus." Mianya looked at me.

"They've got enough going on, Mimi," I said.

"You're right. Trish, thank you. We're gonna catch the bus back to post."

*

When we sat down for the ride I asked Mimi, "Boo, I'm sorry about last night."

"Baby, you can talk to me about it when you're ready. Don't even think about it, OK?"

"OK, Mimi. Are you going to move back in?"

She smiled at me. "I never moved out. That's why you don't have a new roommate. I was just so mad at you I couldn't be around you, Dahni."

"Mimi, you're a drama queen. You made me think—"

"Uh, drama? You got drama too baller. Don't even try it. And by the way, do you know my name yet, partna?" She reminded me about calling her "Sealyn" in the bathroom at TJ's. This was a battle of wits I would not win. That girl had a Tevo in her brain that always knew how to replay my shit to my disadvantage.

"I love you, McPhail." She kissed my cheek and my lips. "So much. I got you, baby, OK? Whatever it is."

Back in our dorm room, we rearranged things to make them a little homier. We moved the wall lockers against the wall so we both could enjoy the space together while we were in there. It was nice enough for now. Mianya went into the bathroom and just as she closed the door, my cell phone rang. It was Sealyn.

"Dahni, I really need to talk to you."

"What's wrong, Sealyn?" I thought the woman was in more danger.

"I just need to talk to you. Please. Can you say you're meeting one of your friends and come downstairs?" She wanted me to lie. I really didn't want to start the lying thing, but I had to go down there and make sure she was OK. I needed to see her with my own eyes.

"OK, I'm on my way." Mianya came out of the bathroom. "Mimi, I'm going to run over to Adrian's room and get my study guide. I'll be back in about thirty minutes."

"OK."

I walked downstairs to meet Sealyn. On the way, I called Adrian so he could back up my story if I needed him to. I just had to remember to come back in the door with a book in my hand. I went to the front door and motioned to Sealyn to drive down to the end of the block. Then I walked down there and got in the car with her. She pulled over into the parking lot corner out of clear view. She was looking much better.

"Sealyn, what's up?"

"Dahni, I am sorry to drag you out here like this but I have to talk to you.

"OK, what's wrong?"

"Do you love me?"

"Sealyn, of course I love you. I love you for the rest of my life. You know that. I can never repay you for what you've done for me."

"No, I mean, do you love me, Dahni? Have you ever felt anything for me? I wrote you a letter and you never responded to it. I should have realized—"

"Wait a minute, Sealyn. Now that you bring that up. . ."

I told Sealyn the whole story surrounding her last letter and the fact that before I read it, I thought she just used me. I told her I knew that she was going to give up everything for me. I let her know that I was no longer mad and I definitely didn't hold anything against her. Simply put, everything for us just happened at the wrong time and it was not her fault or mine but I had her back in any and all things. I also told her that Mianya and I were serious and I was going to deal with her exclusively now.

"I know you and Mianya are kicking it. I wish I knew it was you that she was talking about all those times she was describing her roommate to us. She never once said your name. She's liked you for a long time, Dahni and I respect that. But I've loved you for a longer time and I don't want to lose you again. I'm not staying with T knowing that you are here and there is a chance for us."

"Well, Sealyn. I have to respect my situation with. . ." Sealyn climbed across the console, straddled me, and planted a debilitating kiss on my mouth. Those lips. . . She greedily kissed, nibbled, sucked. . . I tried to resist, but. . .

After what seemed like eternity, she moved back to her seat. "I know you still love me, Dahni. You can't tell me that you don't." I sat in the passenger seat dazed, confused, and hot. FUCK!!! It took almost nothing for this woman to bring me to arousal. *What in the hell was I going to do?*

"Dahni, please give our love another chance."

"Sealyn, I've got to go. Mimi expects me back in a minute."

"I understand, Dahni. I'm not trying to rush you by any means. I understand your situation and everything that you're dealing with. Will you meet me tomorrow so we can fuck?"

"Tomorrow, Sealyn! I can't do that!"

"Meet me early. Before you have to go in to work."

"But Mianya is back in the room! Besides that, I have to study and practice this week. It's impossible!"

"OK, well call me when you can meet me. Dahni, call me when you can, please."

"OK, Sealyn."

"I love you, Dahni."

"I love you too, Sealyn."

"I'll see you tomorrow, baby."

DAMN! Now, I know I just told that woman I couldn't see her tomorrow. I got the book from Adrian, went back up to my room, and went inside.

"Hey, Baby." Mianya hugged me when I came in the door. She kissed me softly, in love and oblivious to my shit.

*

The next few weeks flew by. I managed to do an outstanding job on the sergeant's board and was getting promoted within the next ninety days. Mianya and I were doing very well. I was coming to terms with myself and the Friday incident. TJ was still in rehab but seemed to be getting herself straight, and Sealyn and I were sneaking around and spending every moment we could together. I was a tired, lying mess.

"Sealyn, I can't do this anymore." I said this between kisses. "It's not fair to Mimi." Sealyn had stopped by my and Mianya's room during lunchtime. Mianya was working through lunch this week so I had the space to myself. I was getting really stupid and down right careless with my cheating thing. I needed to get this woman OUT of our room so Mianya wouldn't smell her when she came in later. But Sealyn had some kind of hold over me. Her touch was so good and I was so indebted to her for everything she'd done! She made me so horny.

### Don't Ask, Don't Tell

"Dahni, I want to be with you and only you. My decision is already made. I'm just waiting for you to decide that you want to be with me." Sealyn was driving me crazy with her love. On top of everything else. I was running out of time and running out of options.

"Please Sealyn, you know my situation. You are going to have to stop with the pressure. That's something I can't just up and do right now. Plus you kow you have TJ"

"OK, Dahni. I understand and I heard what you said. But prolonging this situation will only hurt our significant others. This isn't fair to Mianya or TJ." She turned. "Let me use your bathroom right quick."

I sat on the edge of my bed, mentally exhausted. I didn't have a soul to talk to about this. I was alone in my stupid decision making process. I thought about calling Sanders to tell her about it. She would help after she finished cursing. I had a headache. My head was in my hands when the door opened.

"Hey Sweets! What are you doing here?" I stood up looking caught like two mutha fuggas. At that same moment, Sealyn came out of the bathroom. I guessed my run as Casanova was over.

"Mimi!" Sealyn smiled. "What's up, sweetie? I've been trying to call your cell."

"Sealyn?" Mimi did that thing with her eyebrow but the thing was looking kind of evil this time.

"I just left from seeing TJ at the rehab center. Since you're right over here, I came to see why you hadn't called me back." Mimi stepped back and looked at Sealyn.

"I don't have any missed calls."

"Well, I called you, girl. I just dropped by to leave you a note and Dahni walked up when I was leaving. I asked her to use the bathroom."

"Uh, OK." Mimi was still suspicious.

"All I wanted to know was would you help me plan and shop for TJ's 'better than ever' party. She comes home Friday."

Talk about quick on her feet! I meant to never forget that Sealyn was a pro. I'm glad because my shit was shabby. Mimi's heart took over her head.

"TJ gets out this weekend? Oh, thank the Lord!" I was thankful too, but for me. "Sealyn, let's have a dry party. No alcohol whatsoever. We can play games and. . ."

I watched in amazement as the whole situation shifted from my ass being in a sling to planning a coming home get together for TJ. Sealyn worked Mimi's mind like a freaking con artist. I was relieved but the thing I noticed above all else was that this was the first time Sealyn mentioned anything about TJ coming home.  Sealyn hadn't said a word about TJ's release before this very moment.  All she talked about was being with me.  Every conversation was about us being together.  I wondered why Sealyn didn't say anything to me about it.  Well, she probably didn't want me to start tripping.  Sealyn knows how I can be when it comes to her.

"...And girl, I will call you again tonight so we can plan the menu.  Then, I'll come and pick you up early Friday so we can get everything done before twelve hopefully.  She gets released at 5 pm.  I want to be finished decorating and cooking, and have everyone there so she can come in the door to a surprise."  They had a verbal plan on lock.

"Sealyn, this is going to be so much fun.  I'm so happy for you and TJ!" Mimi was beaming from the idea of the party.  She was even happier about the fact that TJ was better and being released.  Mimi was just happy! Me too, 'cause I wasn't caught.

"Girl, I'm hopeful.  I really hope that this is going to be the time TJ gets it together."  Mimi hugged Sealyn, and kissed her on the cheek.

"Everything is going to be fine, sweetie."  Gosh, Mimi is such a nice person.

And everything *was* fine! Yes it was!  Sealyn said her good-byes, left the room and left me standing there amazed by her skill.  I regrouped and grabbed my jacket so I could get back to work on time.

"See you later, baby."  I headed out the door.

"Hold up, partna." Mimi grabbed me by the arm. "Let me talk to you. We need to get something straight. I know you're going through something and I don't want to be tripping with you. You know I'm not a jealous or insecure person, but I don't play this 'you in the room alone with *any* bitch' kind of shit. Please respect me. Sealyn and I are friends but you know we are not friends like that. Friend or no friend, I don't trust anybody--especially a damn fem--alone with my lover. And even worse, someone who is unhappy and in an unstable, abusive relationship who's also feeling nostalgic about yo nigga ass." Mianya got louder and louder. "Nigga, I didn't trip today, because I chose to believe what Sealyn was saying about stopping by to see me for the party. But I don't give a damn what the reason is the next time. You *will* see another side of me if I walk in here or walk up on y'all by yourselves again. Let me make it clear how I feel. If I'm not here, she doesn't come in this room with you alone. Fuck friendship. Do you have a reason to be alone with her, Dahni?"

"No."

"You damn right, 'no.' I give you your respect and all I'm asking you to do is give me mine."

Well, I guess Mianya was not so naïve after all. "I'm sorry, Boo. I really didn't think anything of it."

"It's all good Dahni, but this is your one and only. I'm going to turn this shit out the next time. Just so you know. Don't act surprised when I do it." And then she said sweetly, "I love you, baby. See you later." She hugged and kissed me. I walked out the room and down the hall thinking about everything that just transpired. Thinking about everything. As I went back to work, I acknowledged the fact that I was truly out of my league with this messing around and trying to cheat shit.

## Chapter 16

**Sealyn** called me the next day and explained to me why she didn't tell me about TJ. I was right. She thought I was going to trip and felt I didn't need any additional stress. I guess I do have a rep for not taking things lightly. Later, she stopped by and got some kisses from me as we hid out in the car. A girl who resembled Mianya walked by the car and I almost had a stroke!

"Sealyn, this is the last time we do this stuff. This is reckless."

"That's why it's fun, baby. Anybody could see us, Dahni."

"It ain't fun to me, Sealyn."

"Dahni, I like it spicy. Do you know how many times I just wanted to tell you to go inside my pants and do something to me right here? You have no idea."

"Hello, Sealyn. Is somebody with some got damn sense over there in your head?

Girl, if we get caught doing this shit, my relationship is over. TJ will probably kill you. All kinds of shit will go down."

"But we'll be together."

"Sealyn, I'm not into necrophilia. I ain't trying to get down with a corpse!" We both laughed. "Let me get out of here. See you." I got out of TJ's car. Sealyn pulled off and someone tapped me on the shoulder

"Hey, baby!" A ball of fear nearly choked me where I stood. I swung around expecting to see Michael Friday standing behind me.

"Sanders! You fucking idiot! Dammit! Man, you scared the shit out of me! Don't do that to me, man."

"If you weren't in the car with Sealyn's ho ass you wouldn't have to be so damn nervous. Why are you fucking around with Sealyn. I thought you were done with that?"

"I don't know what you're talking about."

"You *need* to know what I'm talking about. You think people are blind and crazy? Who else around here has a black Audi with a fucking Drill Sergeant hat in the back, idiot? You slippin', dawg."

I thought about what Sanders was saying.

"You better be glad it was me that walked up on you and not TJ or Mimi. Stop pushing it, dude. You act like you have a death wish."

"Wait, what are you doing down here during the week?"

Sanders was down my way for a week of training. Cool. I made it a point to spend time with her so I could get some advice. I could already see what her advice was going to be just by the conversation we'd had so far.

"D, you need to leave Sealyn alone. Just be friends. I'm telling you that for your own good. You know you can't handle that."

"Sanders, I thought you were cool with Sealyn."

"I am cool with her. But you have somebody and she has somebody. Let them work out their situation and you and Mimi work on building y'alls situation back up. You don't need any bullshit." Sanders was right.

"But I still love Sealyn."

"You love the idea of what you and Sealyn could have had. You don't even know Sealyn, Dahni. You don't know her. You still see her as your first and she can do no wrong in your eyes--especially now."

"Whatever, Sanders. I'm not stupid."

"I didn't say you were stupid. All I said is you might not be seeing things clearly. And how do you know if you *ever* even knew Sealyn? You don't, do you? Take care of your household, man. Trust me on this."

## Don't Ask, Don't Tell

I didn't get Sanders. She was right there when Sealyn basically saved my life. Why was she tripping. I felt her, though. I needed to hear what she had to say but I just wasn't ready to accept it.

"Sanders I know what I'm doing where Sealyn is concerned. She has been nothing but honest with me and there for me. She loves me and I love her. We just have to figure out a way to be together."

"Oh really, Dahni? She's been honest with you? The next time you talk to Sealyn ask her why TJ really got drunk and kicked her ass right before Trish made TJ go into rehab. Ask her and come back and tell me. I bet you Sealyn won't tell you that TJ walked in on her and that tall chick Donnetta looking like they were about to fuck or just got finished fucking and TJ whooped every ass in the house. I bet you Sealyn won't tell you that shit! Sealyn is the reason why TJ is crazy, Dahni. TJ needs to leave Sealyn's ho ass alone. It's not the other way around!"

I knew Sanders was wrong because I was at the house that night when Sealyn showed up with the black eye. I shook my head in disbelief as Sanders kept on.

"Sealyn's got everybody thinking that she's all sweet and innocent while she is out here sleeping with everybody behind everybody's back. She's sleeping with eeeeerrrrrrbody, Dahni. Sealyn is a ho, dawg. She is a good friend, not a good girlfriend, man. Didn't she fuck you the first night y'all got together?"

## Dahni McPhail

My mind raced back to that night. We did do it. But that was the first chance we really had to be together! Our passion couldn't wait!

"Quiet is kept, Sealyn slept with Trish. That's why Trish is so guilty and does all the things that she does and that's why Trish can't say anything when Sealyn shows up on her doorstep. Because Trish done been up in her best friend's girlfriend's coodie-coo, Dee. I'm telling you Dahni, you don't know what you're dealing with."

I sat there for a minute and thought about what Sanders was saying. I thought about everything that happened between Sealyn and me. Sealyn would have to be a psychopath to take a lie to that level. I knew she wasn't that! Then I thought back on how Sanders was always trying to be up in Sealyn's face when we were in basic training. That's when it dawned on me. Sanders wanted Sealyn! Sanders was probably just hating. She did get sarcastic about me "having two beautiful girls" and it not being a real problem. She was jealous of Sealyn and me. Sanders was a hater!

I kept my thoughts to myself and thanked Sanders for being so up front with me. Then I let that crap go in one ear and out the other. She was wrong about Sealyn. Look how The Jackal treated us in basic. That's exactly how TJ was treating Sealyn, now. And that bullshit about Trish and Sealyn. Neither one of them would ever do a thing like that! Sanders was wrong. No one could tell me about Sealyn. She was there when I needed her most. I knew her better than anyone else!

*

## Don't Ask, Don't Tell

The weekend came and Mianya was busy helping Sealyn get things together all day long. I thought I was going to get a break and just chill out, but Mimi left a list of things for me to complete while she was working on the party. No rest for the weary.

I finished my duties and caught up with Sanders as instructed. Bri and Diana were waiting for us over at Di and Trish's house. Once I arrived, we were all going to head over to Sealyn and TJ's from there. No sooner than I closed the passenger door of Sanders' car, she started.

"Well?" I knew what she was talking about.

"Well, what?"

"You know what I'm talking about, Dahni. Did you ask Sealyn? I saw you with her, Dahni, so you can't say you didn't see her again this week."

"I didn't get the chance to mention it to her. Well, I didn't want to mention it because of everything that was going on this week. I didn't want to ruin her mood."

"OK, *ruin her mood*. Your relationship is going to be ruined. I'm not saying another word about it. You wanna mess up everything you have, that's on you." *Thank you for deciding not to say anything else about it.* "But when the shit hits the fan. . ." *I thought you weren't going to say anything else.* ". . .don't say I didn't tell you!"

I had to love my dawg, Sanders. She seemed truly concerned about my welfare. I told her, "I got this," and I was being careful. She reminded me that she saw me with Sealyn and that I was not being careful. I was happy to be hanging with Sanders, but I was glad to get the hell out of that car when we got to Trish's.

Bri came out to meet us. "Hey baby." She hugged and kissed Sanders. I forgot they hadn't seen each other for over a week. "Hey Dahni, sweetie." I gave Bri a hug.

"Mimi in there, Bri?"

"No, she's over at TJ's house still." I looked at my watch. "I guess she's gonna get dressed over there. Are we leaving here any time soon? I have Mimi's clothes."

"We're leaving in about five minutes," Di said. Trish has already gone to pick up TJ. She should be getting to the rehab center right about now."

"OK. Bet. Who's driving?"

"Me." Diana came out the house. "Go ahead and drink your beer and your shots now because there is not going to be any liquor, beer or anything in the house or around the party—period. TJ needs all the support she can get." I wondered why Diana thought that Sanders and I were trying to get our buzz on before we got to the party. We were planning to do that, but I just wonder how Diana knew. Sanders looked at me.

"Let's not drink anything, Dahni. We can wait until the party's over and we get back here."

"Yeah, you're right." As much as I despised The Jackal, I still couldn't stand for anyone to be as bad off as she was right about now. The fact that she didn't sign herself out of rehab early and accepted some help with her problem showed that she was trying. When I thought about it, I figured The Jackal was probably boozing on those days she tried to kill us. "Yeah, Sanders. She does need our support."

We loaded up in the Range Rover and drove over to the house. We all walked in and greeted each other with hugs. Then our mouths dropped open. Why? Because the house was awesome. They did a house transformation like on the home improvement shows. Purple, silver and black. It was set up like a house concert with a stage for a performer and a seating area out in front.

"Because TJ is going to be the star of the show tonight!" Mimi was so excited.

Ninety percent of the decorations and the set up was Mianya's work because she was good at that stuff. That's why Sealyn asked for her help in the first place. Mimi could take a few items and put them in a basket with some colored wrap and it would look like you bought it at the store.

She had that house looking fantastic! Everyone was impressed and excited.

Mimi came up to me and kissed me. "Do you like it, baby?"

"Girl, you're gonna make us rich one day, Mimi. You've really outdone yourself." I saw Sealyn looking at us. Then, I saw Sanders looking at us all.

"Baby thank you!" Mimi was going through her bag, smiling at me. "You remembered everything I asked for! Even the right colored lip liner! Sealyn, I told you my baby had everything on lock. I knew she was going to bring me what I needed." So, they've been talking about me today, huh?

Mimi went upstairs and got dressed. I followed her so I could get some love. I grabbed her and started groping her while she was taking off her clothes. "Stop, silly!" I wrapped my arms around her and held her close to me. Then I kissed her. She was so good to me and so good to everyone around her. I didn't deserve her and she definitely didn't deserve my cheating ass.

"What, Dahni?"

"Nothing. Thank you, Mimi. And I love you. That's all."

"I'm in this, OK? Now, can I get dressed before Trish and TJ get here?"

## Don't Ask, Don't Tell

"OK, baby." Mimi put on her clothes and once again, she was PAI YOW! Fine as all get out. That girl knows she looks good, got damn! She had on her skinny jeans with her black "ho" boots with the three-inch heels and a black button down shirt. She wore her hair down tonight. Simple but mmmm... Sexaaaaaayyyy! Time to get downstairs and get ready for the arrival of the guest of honor!

By now, the house was packed and everyone was commenting on how beautiful things were. Mimi graciously gave Sealyn all the credit—and Sealyn took the credit too. Diana shouted, "They're coming!" Everybody parked down the street and around the corners, so no cars were in the yard. We planned to surprise the hell out of TJ when she stepped in the door.

And that's exactly what happened--in reverse. *WE* got the surprise! When the door opened, Trish walked in with some other woman. Then we realized it was The Jackal! Everybody screamed. It was like The Jackal had gone to extreme makeover. She looked great! Sanders looked at me. We both were thinking the same thing. Fuckin' alcohol was making The Jackal look that fucked up? Her caramel skin was smooth and clear. Her eyes were grey, the whites were white, and she didn't look like the devil. Her hair looked thick, full and was down past her shoulders. She looked so good. Diana, Bri, and Mianya busted out crying. They ran over to her hugging and kissing TJ.

"Let her in the house, y'all."

TJ walked in the house to more hugs and kisses. Cameras flashed and tears fell. Everyone really loved TJ and wanted to see her well. That confused me. Wasn't TJ the bad guy?

TJ walked through the house and went up to Sealyn. Trish moved them to the stage area. It was like a reality show. TJ and Sealyn hugged and kissed. It was so touching. I wasn't mad because I knew Sealyn had to front. Then, to everyone's surprise, TJ got on one knee.

"Baby, I know that we have gone through our ups and downs but I really love you. Getting sober made me realize what I have in you. I don't want to lose your love for any reason. I am focused on keeping my life together and committing myself to making things work out with you."

I looked at Sanders. Sanders had this weird "oh no" type of look on her face. "I want to be with you forever, baby. Will you marry me, Sealyn?"

All the girly girls in the house screamed and jumped around hugging each other. The cameras flashed again. There was more applause and hugs. Diana, Bri and Mimi were crying again. I just stood there because I was shocked. That wasn't it, though. There was more to come.

Sealyn bent down, kissed TJ and said, "Tamika Jones, I have never loved anyone in my life as much as I love you. You are everything to me and there is no other. I want to dedicate my life to making sure that you are well, that you are loved, and that you are taken care of. My heart belongs to you. I know that you asked me to marry you but," Sealyn pulled TJ to her feet and then got down on one knee, "Tamika, will you do me the undeserved honor of marrying me?"

I mentally nic-named Bri, Di, and Mimi "the Emotions" for all the damn crying. I thought we were going to have to sedate those three. Makeup ran down cheeks. They were overjoyed. Everybody was. The kisses, hugs, pictures, and congratulations were going around again. The sparkling grape juice toasts were flowing. I figured the next party would be in Amsterdam for the wedding. It was a real nice situation except for the fact that just yesterday Sealyn asked me when I was going to make a decision about her and me. If that information weren't in my head, I probably would have enjoyed the proposals as much as everybody else did.

"I told you that bitch was an actress. See how good she flipped that shit? Could you have thought of something as fast as she just did? Sealyn is a chameleon, Dahni, a fucking chameleon. No matter what she did for you, you cannot keep fucking with her." Sanders came behind me and was whispering in my ear. "Leave that bitch alone today!"

My dawg. I might have thought Sanders was lying and trying to hate with all the other things she said about Sealyn, but I just saw this woman switch gears like a race car driver—and on the fly, no less. I could dismiss the rest, but there was no way I could dispute my own eyes.

*

There also was no way that I could dispute my own ears when my phone rang and it was a call from Mobile, Alabama. The city and state from which Michael Friday hailed. I hardly believed my ears. I started not to answer the phone but I decided to take ownership of the rest of my peace, curse this crazy motherfucker out, threaten his career and life and ensure that he left me alone once and for all. It wasn't Michael on the other end of the phone though.

"Its Reggie." Michael's brother. I hoped he wasn't calling me to try to get me and Mike back together.

"DeeDee, Michael never showed up to his new unit."

"Um, OK." Sealyn's friend put Mike on emergency orders within a week of the incident and I hadn't heard from him since. As far as I knew, he was in the states pretending to be an outstanding Soldier at his new unit. I had no idea of his whereabouts. But I quickly started to become interested in his location.

"He came home on leave and then went to report to Fort Polk, DeeDee. He signed in at the post but he never showed up to process into his new company. That was over six months ago.

"Wow. Really? You think he went AWOL?" Fear crept up my legs and into my heart. I immediately prayed to God that Mike wasn't back over here in Germany trying to catch up with me.

### Don't Ask, Don't Tell

"The Criminal Investigative Division searched for him since he went missing because he left his car on post with all his belongings in it."

My heart sank.

"A week ago, the Army Corps of Engineers began…" Reggie's voice cracked. "Began digging up old wells on the outskirts of Fort Polk and found the remains of a Soldier in one of the wells. The remains were identified as Michael's. He's dead, DeeDee. Someone murdered him and stuffed his body down inside the well."

I was almost ashamed of myself for the feeling of relief that washed over my body at the news. I no longer had to look over my shoulder or worry that one day he would be coming around the next corner. Michael Friday was dead and the details of his death were disturbing. Michael's killer cut off his penis and shoved it down his throat. The coroner found a broken beer bottle inside his anus. He was tortured for hours and then stuffed him the well alive. Almost every bone in his body was broken.

"Damn, Reggie. That is all the way fucked up. I'm so sorry to hear that."

Even though Michael dogged me, there was not one portion of my heart that wanted something this awful to happen to him. In hindsight, I know that Mike was emotionally immature and couldn't handle our situation. He wasn't strong enough to believe that I actually was going to stay with him and my heart had long forgiven him for the Friday incident. I was mortified hearing all that happened to him and that he was tortured to death. God rest his soul.

# Dahni McPhail

When I told San what happened to Mike, even she had to show some sympathy. "Got damn, Dahni!" That shit was just off the chain. San reported Mike's death to Sealyn and told me about her reaction.

"Sealyn heard the news, Dahni, and kept it moving. She didn't care." I wasn't surprised.

I hadn't spoken to her in a while. I was actually relieved that Sealyn didn't wasn't bothering me and was glad that San took it upon herself to inform Sealyn about Mike's death.

When I thought about it, the last time I'd seen or dealt with Sealyn was at the proposal fiasco. And that was good. The Jackal and Sealyn went to Amsterdam and got married. Trish threw the reception for them at the Lofthouse. Mimi did the decorations and I rocked the guests. Everything was lovely and life was getting back to normal. Better than normal for Tamika Jones.

The sober TJ was a lot more user friendly than the drunken Jackal. I spent a lot of time talking with her when we were "shooed" out of the way while Mimi and the other chicks decorated for the reception and other events of the last few weeks. She was really a nice person and didn't remember half the things she did while she was drunk. The difference between her two personalities was baffling. This person was kind, funny, nice and so generous. She would do anything for you. Fine as shit, too—the exact opposite of the crazy drunk. Yeah. She told me she was drunk the whole while we were in basic training. She asked for my forgiveness. I forgave her for it and gave my drill sergeant a hug.

Now, TJ was determined to stay in control of her life from here on out and determined to make a happy home for herself and her partner. Inside, I hoped that Sealyn wouldn't do anything that would fuck it up and drive TJ back to the bottle.

I hoped for too much. Sealyn hadn't missed a beat. Sanders pointed out the new chick that Sealyn was messing around with. *How did Sanders keep up with all this stuff anyway?* "Yeah, dog. Watch her. If you watch Sealyn, you will learn a whole lot. She got more game than you, me and everybody else put together." The new conquest was a chick named Kelly. Diana introduced Kelly to the gang. She was a friend of Di's from another duty station. She was cool and fit right in. Everybody liked Kelly.

"Yeah, Kelly's cool but Sealyn's fucking with her. You think I'm playing? You wanna see?" Sanders walked past Diana into the kitchen and picked up her car keys. "Sabrina, Dahni and I are going to run to the store and get some beer. You want anything back?"

"Wine, please. Not everybody wants to drink beer, woman!" Sanders laughed.

"Anybody else?"

"Mimi, do you want anything, love muffin?" I asked. Mimi laughed. I make her happy.

"Dahni get some of those sweet potato chips we tried the other day so everyone can taste them. They were good!" They *were* good.

"OK, I'll get enough for everybody." I walked over and gave Mimi a hug and a kiss. She hugged me back a little longer than I expected. "What's up, boo?"

"Nothing. I love you."

"I love you too Mianya McPhail."

*

"Look over there, dog. What do you see?" We were riding down Reicherstrasse and I saw the black Audi. "I told you Sealyn ain't shit. She's going to drive TJ crazy again because she's going to keep fuckin' around openly until she gets caught. Sealyn is like a daredevil. Look how she just parks the car right out in clear view and doesn't care." Sanders pulled her car into a parking space. "Come on."

I followed Sanders so I could see Sealyn in action, but I was a little hurt, a little amazed, a little bothered. I felt all kinds of emotions. Confirming that I really was a just a conquest wasn't fun at all. My first experience with sex and being in love with a woman and I was just a conquest for that ho ass ho. I was glad I had Mimi, but it still hurt. We went into an apartment building and walked up to a door. "Listen." I couldn't hear at first, but then I heard that familiar sound and that familiar voice. Sealyn was getting laid. I looked up at Sanders and my eyes filled with tears. Sanders looked surprised.

"Aw, shit. Let's get out of here. I forgot about you and your punk ass feelings." Sealyn easily made me cry. I barely made it back to Sanders' car before I broke down in tears. I don't know why I cried so much and hurt so bad. I knew it was stupid of me to cry about it. That knowledge didn't help me stop the tears from falling, though.

"Hey, I'm sorry dawg. If I knew you were going to react like that, I would never have taken you in there. I thought you were finally seeing Sealyn like I see her after the proposal bullshit and the wedding bullshit. The girl is just a ho and a pathological liar. She has fooled TJ into thinking that TJ, herself, is wrong for being upset with her for cheating. You know, Dahni, I've been trying to figure out how you even got into Sealyn in the first place knowing that we all slept with her in basic training."

"What did you say, Sanders?"

"I said I don't know how you fell in love with Sealyn knowing that Me, Howard, Benson, and Dorsey slept with Sealyn while we were in basic training."

"Well, I *didn't* know."

That bit of information was just a little too much for me. I put my head in my hands and started bawling hard. "Oh my freakin' God!

Dahni, you didn't know that we all hit that? Dahni, please tell me you knew." Sanders pulled the car over again, jumped out and came around on my side. She opened the door, wrapped her arms around me and held me. She was crying now, herself. "Dahni, I am a crazy ass but I would have never, ever told you the shit like that if I thought you didn't know. All this time, you didn't know. It all makes sense to me now. Oh my God, I'm so sorry! D, I'm so sorry"

Sanders apologized for everything from telling me about the letter to telling me anything about Sealyn. Sanders assumed I knew about all the other shit and thought that I just liked sleeping with Sealyn, slipped and caught feelings or got caught up since Sealyn was so good in bed. Sanders had no idea I was totally in the dark about everything and Sealyn was playing me like I meant so much to her because she was my first. She was the first lesbian experience for everybody, even the girls that were with The Kru in the hotel room that night. Sealyn had slept with us all! Bitch!

## Chapter 17

We were out at "the store" a whole lot longer than anyone expected us to be. I had to get myself together and come up with a reason why my eyes were looking like someone dropped hot sauce in them before I went back in that house.

"Damn, did you make the wine?" Bri is a nut and that is why she and Sanders are perfect for each other.

"Yeah," Sanders replied, "and you know how long it took me to press the grapes the last time so I don't even know why you're complaining!" We all laughed. Yes. Laughter was what I needed.

"T called here for Sealyn. Have y'all heard from her?" Mimi asked. Then a look of concern came across her face. "Dahni, what's wrong with your eyes?"

"I don't know, Boo. We got on post and I just started sneezing like crazy. I put some of this up my nose." I pulled out some allergy medicine that Sanders told me to buy. Sanders was on it, man.

"You're going to see the doctor Monday." Mimi gave me a serious look.

"K. I'm about to drink this beer now, though. What did you guys cook?"

We ate and had a few drinks and settled in to watch a movie. We were at the good part when the house phone rang. Diana got up to find the phone and answer it. It was T. "Trish, T is still looking for Sealyn. She hasn't come home yet or called or anything." Trish jumped to her feet and ran to get the phone from Diana. "T hung up, baby," Diana said just as Trish reached her.

"How did she sound, Di? Did she sound like she was drinking?" Trish put on her Timbs and brushed her hair back into a ponytail.

"She didn't sound like she was drinking, baby. She was just wondering if Sealyn was here."

"I'm going over there." Trish started toward the door.

"Go with her, Dahni." Mimi was up in arms now. "You go too, baby." Bri, Diana and Mimi were going to wait at the apartment for Sealyn just in case she showed up.

Shit, Sanders and I knew where the bitch was. As soon as the car door closed, Sanders said, "Trish, Sealyn is over at Kelly's fucking. That's what took us so long because we saw T's car out in front of the apartment building." Trish's face turned from concern to rage.

## Don't Ask, Don't Tell

"I'll kill that whore tonight just as sure as my name is—"

"Kill her for what, Trish?" This time I was the voice of reason. "We should just show T the shit so she will finally leave Sealyn's ass alone for good and get with someone who deserves a nice person." *Did I just say that about The Jackal?* "Sealyn ain't worth anyone going to jail."

We got to the house and found T pacing the floor with a worried look on her face. Trish went in first and hugged T—very relieved that T was sober. "Have you heard anything from her?" Trish was faking concern. I wanted to just say where the bitch was but my heart ain't hard like that. T had been through enough.

"No. This is not the norm for her, Trish. She'll usually call or something. She has her cell phone with her." I got on my cell phone and called Mianya's number trying to feign concern.

"Mimi, baby. Did she contact you guys yet?"

"Dahni, we're with her right now. I was just getting ready to call you. Sealyn caught a flat tire and realized that she'd left her cell phone at home. So she's been out here for hours trying to flag down someone to help her. Somebody finally stopped and let Sealyn use their cell phone. She couldn't get through on anyone's number then she tried me, got through and we came out here to get her." I looked at T.

"Mimi's with Sealyn now. Sealyn caught a flat. Baby, put her on the phone so T can talk to her." I handed T my phone. T was relieved.

"Baby, I was so worried about you!"

I hoped what I was feeling wasn't on my face. I was mad at that lying, conniving ass ho tonight like I hadn't ever been mad at anything or anyone before in my life. We were at home chilling and Sealyn was out there sleeping around. Why the fuck did she have to drag all of us out of our comfort zones and willfully inject us into her scenario to save her lying bitch ass and validate her story? Why? For what?

We got TJ together and drove out to the site. Trish, Sanders, and I were looking at that ho Sealyn like we wanted to kill her ass when we got out there to the car. Sealyn, crying a river of fake tears, jumped into TJ's arms as soon as she saw her. This ho was on another level. Sealyn was WAY beyond anything I had ever seen in my life. She was more than a pimp or a player. She was the grand orchestrator. I watched as my, Sanders' and Trish's girlfriends hugged and comforted this charlatan. Now I understood perfectly why TJ was beating Sealyn's ass down during her drinking stage. TJ wasn't crazy at all. She had—in my eyes—a legitimate excuse. I wouldn't hit a woman, but I wanted to beat Sealyn's ho ass out there that night on the fucking autobahn in the damn dark with cars flying by at a hundred miles an hour. This bitch had done flattened her own fucking tire just to add to her story. The next time TJ jumped on her, I was going to help.

*

That shit last weekend really burned my ass. I was still mad about it a whole seven days later. I had never seen anything to top Sealyn's act.

## Don't Ask, Don't Tell

Not even in a movie. I mean, this was real life and I hadn't seen a movie actor who could top Sealyn's show out there on the highway. That girl didn't give a shit about anything except getting off the hook.

"Dahni, please stop slamming drawers. What in the world is wrong? Did something happen today at work?" Was I slamming drawers? "Regardless of what happened at work, it's Friday and its time to get ghost. Quit trippin'. Gimme a kiss." Mianya was not trying to have a bad time this weekend. I didn't blame her. We'd had enough drama to last a lifetime. Lesbians, I mean my family, sure can be dramatic.

It was festival time. The fest was the German equivalent to a carnival, but way better, and we were all going out to have fun, eat some good German food, play games and ride some rides. The "fest" grounds were right down the street from Trish's place so we all walked. No need for a designated driver tonight. Everybody could have a cocktail!

"TJ and Sealyn are going to meet us at the front gate." Diana was talking to Mimi.

"They are?" Kelly asked. She was walking with us. Kelly didn't know that Sanders, Trish and I knew why she asked that question. I looked at Sanders then I looked at Trish.

"Trish, is T going to be alright around all this drinking tonight? You know how the fests are." Everybody at the fest usually was drunk—no kidding.

"Dahni, TJ is determined to be successful. She's not even fazed. I'm really proud of her." Trish smiled.

We met them at the gate and started walking around the fest to see what was out there. I was at the fest for one reason and one reason alone. Food. "I don't know how you can just continue to eat and eat and eat like that, Dahni." Mimi said I was making her stomach upset.

"Like this baby. I put the food in my mouth. Then I chew it. Then I swallow it. Then I go to the next food vendor and get more and start the process over."

Mimi cut me a look. "Not funny, Piggy."

We were having a great time. The fest was always a blast. Everyone except T was lit from drinking beer, shots, and wine, and all that drinking had its affect. We had to pee. The bathroom trailer was pretty much empty. Mimi and the other girls went in first. I held everybody's things and stood out there talking to T. After a few minutes, Mimi came out of the trailer with this look on her face. It was a crazy look. "Mimi, what's wrong?"

"Nothing. I'll tell you when we get back home." I wasn't going to forget either.

We'd walked around the festival grounds about three times and I could not fit any more food into my stomach. It was humanly impossible. Everybody else was pretty much in the same condition, plus fucked up. We decided to call it a night and leave. TJ and Sealyn said they were going to give Kelly a ride home. Mianya got that look on her face again. What was wrong with the woman?

I couldn't wait to get by ourselves so I could ask Mimi what was the matter. "Dahni, when I came out of the bathroom stall, that trifling ho Sealyn was kissing Kelly. She tried to lie like she wasn't but I know what I saw. That bitch is going to make TJ start drinking again. I knew she hadn't stopped her whoring around." Mimi was on fire! "She could at least have some respect for TJ. Just the simple common courtesy you would have for a dog! I could have been TJ coming out of that stall or TJ could have been walking in the door! Sealyn is a crazy, hurtful, sleazy, and sneaking around bitch!" I couldn't do anything but agree with that.

"Mimi, You look cute when you're mad like this." I sat on the edge of the bed. Mimi looked like she was going to keep fussing, but she stopped in her tracks. Then she laughed and walked over to me.

"Cute? How about sexy?" She kissed me. "Don't you think I'm sexy, Dahni?" She kissed me again. "Hmm?" Mimi stepped between my legs and squatted down to my level. "I think you're sexy, D. Dahni McPhail." She stood up, took her shirt off, and put her breast in my mouth. "Do you like that?" I sucked her nipple softly. She grabbed my head and pushed it into her breast. "Suck it like you mean it!" I obeyed my mistress and sucked harder. She pulled away from me and stuffed the other one in my mouth. I like it so much when she drinks vodka and cranberry. The bad girl enters the building.

Mimi pushed me off her again and began dancing out of the rest of her clothes. "You want some of this? Come in the shower and get it." We went in the shower and soaped up. Mimi was winding on me while we were wet and soapy. This let me know that she was gonna get her freak on tonight and, yes, I was there to tap that ass! I could see that in her eyes. We rinsed off the soap and she took my hand and walked me out of the shower. She went into her bag and pulled out a plastic penis with belts on it. "Put this on. I bought it for us."

"Wh... how?"

"Oh shit. I forgot you're a baby." She put the "strap" (as she called it) on me. It fit tight and snug. I looked down.

"Why'd you get me this little wee-wee? The other boys are going to tease me in the locker room."

She laughed. "You're so silly. Baby, I don't like a big one. That's more than enough. I'm tight." She looked up at me. "Do you want me to suck it?" I wanted to ask her what the hell I was going to get out of watching her suck something I couldn't feel. But I didn't say anything. I didn't want to mess up her mood.

Mianya stood up, grabbed my head and kissed the hell out of me. She deep throated me with her tongue. Then the freaky church girl started sucking my nipples. The way she acted was making me hawt! I felt the wetness between my legs. Her talented mouth teased my body while her hands explored every place I had skin. She got on her knees in front of me and I thought she was going to suck the plastic thing, but she didn't. She slid her tongue underneath the base of it and dove directly into my hot place. I got nervous and my heart was about to pound out of my chest but I let her do it. I had to let my baby have me this time. And she did. It seemed like her tongue was so long and strong. She moved the strap to the side and began tasting my lips. She was sucking and licking the things that turned me on the most. Damn, it was good. She grabbed my thighs and pulled me closer to her while her tongue kept darting in and out of my folds. I opened my legs to receive her tongue and held back a moan. She knew that she was making me feel good. Her hot strong instrument went around and around on my clit making me feel a throbbing sensation. I knew it wasn't going to be long before I couldn't take anymore. Mimi knew too. She dove into my mound and began loving me with her lips and tongue like there was nothing else on earth. I couldn't fight that. My dam burst. Wetness ran down my legs as I throbbed and pulsed. I grabbed Mimi's head and held on for dear life thinking that I should have let Mimi do this shit a long time ago. She was so good at it. I looked down at the top of Mimi's jet-black hair. She looked up at me and said, "Now come over here and make me scream."

I'd never done the strap thing before but I'd seen enough porn that I wasn't stupid. She walked over to the chair and bent over it. She turned her head toward me. "Get over here!"

Then I said, "Oh, you want some of this, huh?" That was the first time "lil man," my alter ego, showed up in the bedroom. I ran over to her. She raised her eyebrow because I moved so quickly. "You want this dick? Huh? I positioned my "penis" for entry and eased it into her.

"Uuuunngh, Dahni, wait!"

"Naw. Hell no. You were talking shit. You wanted it!" I started pounding her and trying to make her regret ever talking all that trash to me. "Didn't you ask for it?"

"Yes! Baby yes! Oh!"

"Well you're gonna get it then!" I grabbed her hair, put my hand on her back, and went to work.

"Ah... oh yes! Aaaahh. Aaaahh, please!" I beat the brakes off that ass! "Dahni, please!" I started smacking her ass.

"Don't beg me now, Mimi. Mianya (wham!) Don't (wham!) beg (wham!) now (wham!). I was having fun. Mimi was grabbing a hold of anything she could get her hands on, knocking shit off the chair. It was good and the best thing about it was there was a little thing on the penis that was rubbing my clit at the same time I was stroking her. I was getting ready to come again. The more I thrust against her, the more it massaged me. The better it felt, the more I really wore that ass out.

"Dahni, I'm coming! Dahhhhhnnniiiiiiii!" Making love to someone as sexy as Mianya and hearing her screaming your name would break down even the hardest person. When she started coming, so did I.

"Uh... Mimi... .ssssssss... mmmm, girl" She bounced on my rod. We fell into the throes of ecstasy together. Yes! Yes! Yes! BOI YOW! Shit, that was awesome. I collapsed on Mimi's back for a few minutes.

"Mimi?"

"Yes, baby," she panted.

"I'm tired as hell. How do men do this shit all the time? I need oxygen."

"Shut it up, Dahni. You are so silly!"

## Chapter 18

I woke up the next morning and Mimi was not in the bed. Instinctively, I started looking for a note. Then I remembered that I was dealing with Mianya, not that other chick. I washed up and went downstairs to check and see if Mimi was cooking. She and Diana were sitting at the table drinking coffee.

"Good morning, lay-tees," I sang.

"Good morning, bay bay! Das my daddy right there, Di!" Was this woman down here talking with Diana about our sex?

"Morning Dahni. Your plate is in the microwave."

"Where's Trish?" I didn't see her anywhere. "T called her. She's on her way back now."

"Is everything OK?"

"Yeah. No drama this morning." I went to get my plate and Diana and Mimi continued talking.

"Girl, why didn't you say something right then and there?"

"Diana, you know T would have turned the fest completely out and been in jail last night. I thought of the greater good. T is doing so well. I'm just hoping that, in her continued sobriety, she will get strong enough to see the light, leave Sealyn and still be able to deal with life without drinking. I don't want T to relapse. She's come so far."

"T should just beat her again," I said and laughed as I was eating.

"Alright Ms. Celie." Diana and Mianya laughed at me. I was serious as hell, though.

"All these years T has been dealing with Sealyn and her shit and still sticking with her, putting her through college, trying to make a life? Mimi, do some shit like that to me if you dare. You're gonna be the three legged woman because I'm going to leave my whole leg lodged in your ass!" Up went the eyebrow.

"Just remember that it goes both ways, ball-la. It goes both ways." Mimi sucked her teeth.

"T does not need to fight for any reason anymore."

"I know, Di. Don't pay silly any attention. Dahni doesn't mean what she's saying."

"Hmph. Think I don't," I mumbled into my food. I meant that shit with all my heart.

Trish walked in the door with some flowers for Diana. "Baby, the guy was selling them on the side of the strasse. Aren't they pretty?"

"Yes. Thank you, Trish. They really are nice." Di hugged her partner.

"What was T doing, Trish? They coming over?" I asked.

"Yeah, they're coming over later. T had to go in to work for a few hours but she will be home around 2:30 to pick up Sealyn. After that, they're coming through."

"Cool."

Mimi and I got dressed and went back out to the fest because I wanted another kabob and some mushrooms and onions. She went even though she thought something was wrong with me for still wanting food. We got back to the house around 3:00. I expected T and Sealyn to be there.

"Are they still coming?"

"Yeah. Actually, they should be here by now. T is probably getting changed." Another hour went by and still no T and Sealyn. Just then, I heard my cell phone vibrate. I'd left it on the coffee table. I had one message from Sanders and four text messages from Sealyn. I checked the voice message. Sanders just called to see if everybody was OK. Then I checked the texts. They were crazy. They didn't say anything. There was a bunch of gibberish. Then, as I was looking at the phone, Sealyn sent another crazy message that looked just like the rest.

"Mimi, look at this." I gave Mianya the phone and she looked at me.

"What kind of mess is this chick trying to send to you so you can translate it? You know what? Let me call this ho right now. I'm not even trying to play today." Oh, Lord. I should have never even shown it to her.

Mianya called Sealyn's phone. I guess Sealyn answered. Mimi was like "Sealyn look, I don't know what you're trying to do but," she paused. Then Mimi got a petrified look on her face. "Oh my God! Sealyn! Sealyn!" Sealyn must have answered. "Sealyn stay on the phone! Stay on the phone, baby!" *Baby?* What the hell? Mimi was trying to calm Sealyn down.

"What's wrong, Mianya? Trish! Come here!" Mimi kept speaking intensely into the phone. "Tell her it's me, Sealyn. Tell T its Mimi!" By that time, we all were yelling at Mimi to tell us what was going on, but Mimi was still coaching Sealyn. Then Mimi took a second and said, "T came home early and caught Sealyn in the bed with Kelly at 2 o'clock this afternoon. T pulled a glock, started drinking and has held them gunpoint since then! T is drunk right now and going off with a loaded 9 in her hand!" Then Mimi screamed a blood-curdling scream. "Oh my God! T just shot Kelly! I just heard T shoot Kelly! Oh God, she's making Sealyn hang up the phone!"

## Chapter 19

"Diana, send the Polezei over there right now! You and Mimi stay put. Come on, Dahni!" We jumped in the BMW and sped across town breaking every traffic law in the land. Trish skidded to a stop leaving the car on the sidewalk and half way in the street. She used her key to get in.

"Oh no! Oh no, T!" When we walked in the door, there was blood on the wall with a streak running down to the floor. Kelly was lying on the floor with a hole in her head. She was dead. We carefully walked in a little further. "Tamika! Tamika this is Patricia!"

"Get the fuck out of here, Trish!" T was crying. "Get out of here! This is between me and Sealyn!"

"Tamika, please. Please just let me talk to you." We walked in and T was sitting on the couch, in uniform, with an almost empty bottle in her right hand and a gun in her left. Sealyn was naked and cowering over by the big screen TV. Sealyn looked at Trish.

"Trish, help me."

T jumped up. "Bitch, you didn't need no help when you were fucking that mothefucker in my bed, did you?" T pointed the gun at Sealyn. "Get yo goat smelling ass up, bitch!" T grabbed Sealyn up and threw her against the wall near us.

"Tamika, put the gun down, please. Please don't ruin your entire life!" T looked at Trish.

"Trish, my fucking life is over! Kelly is dead. Kelly is dead. I killed Kelly! Oh God, I killed Kelly!" T was drunk and rambling. She sat down again and continued crying. Sealyn attempted to move and T pointed the gun at her. "Stop, bitch. Move another step! Move and I'll kill you right fucking now!"

It was a scene out of a crime show. Trish was trying to reason with T. Sealyn was crying, naked and shaking. I was scurred than a mutha fugga. I mean this was for real bullets flying shit. A dead woman was in the other room and the person who killed her was still in here drunk and waving a loaded weapon. I thought that some chaos would happen when T caught Sealyn again (because we knew that was coming), but I just never imagined anything like this. And where was the damn Polezei? If we were playing the music too loudly, they'd be here by now.

Tears streamed down Trish's face as the pleaded with Tamika to put down the gun and stop right now before things got any worse. Then I heard familiar voices in the distance.

## Don't Ask, Don't Tell

"Kelly! Oh my God, Kelly!" Diana and Mianya were at the door screaming. Now, didn't we tell them to stay their asses put?

"Get out of here. Go outside Mianya! Go! Get the fuck outside both of you!" I shouted.

Mianya screamed my name. "Dahni! Dahni!" Diana was screaming for Trish.

"We're OK. Just go outside, baby, and don't come back in. Diana, Mianya, please listen to me. Please go outside. Just go. We got this. Get some help." I was a damn lie. *We ain't "got" shyt!*

I turned my attention back to the scene in front of me where T was talking like she was truly and completely insane. I looked in her eyes and saw that Sergeant First Class Tamika Jones was mentally gone. "You slept with my cousin, Sealyn. With my brother. You got pregnant by my brother and I still stayed with you. After I accepted it and still wanted the baby, you got an abortion and didn't tell me. You slept with people at my job. At your college. Through everything, I stayed with you. Bitch, I damn near drank myself to death over you. Now, after all the shit you have done to me. I come into the house that I got so that we could be together. . .," she trailed off. T's eyes seemed like they turned black. "I risked my career to marry you." She raised the gun and Sealyn screamed. Hearing Sealyn, Mianya and Diana started screaming outside. "And I come in here today to find you in OUR bed with this motherfucker here?" T fired another shot into Kelly. Diana and Mimi were now officially out of their minds with fear. They were screaming and crying their lungs out in the front yard. And, oh by the way, now, I was completely scared shitless.

"Tamikaaaaaaaaa!!!! Tamika!!!! Stooooop!" Trish screamed at the top of her lungs. T lifted the gun. I saw her finger pulling the trigger. All I could think to do was try to push Sealyn out of the way. BANG! *Oh fuck! My drill sergeant has finally killed me.*

*I'm dead*, I thought as I fell on the floor. I heard Sealyn scream again. Mianya and Diana were still screaming in the distance. Then Trish screamed again! "Tamikaaaaaaaaa! Stop! Nooooo!" I heard one more shot, a thump, then a muffled shot and another thump. Then I heard nothing but Trish's sobs. "No! Mik, no! No, no, no, no! Why didn't you just leave? Why didn't you just leave her? Mik? Get up, Mik. Get up. Please Get uuuuu uuuu uu uuuppp." Trish sounded like she lost her best friend.

My chest was on fire. I want my Mommy! Mooommmyyyy! This shit is painful. Somebody get my Mommy. Finally, the pain just stopped. I sat on the chandelier and watched as Mianya rushed in the room and let out the kind of scream that comes from the soul. She dropped to her knees, shaking me. Crying. Then, she got on the phone. Calling. Trying to get help for me. But I was dead. Just like I told you earlier.

I saw the police and the paramedics arrive. "Move! Everybody out! Get them out of the way!" Now, the authorities were screaming. "Commander, we have two fatalities, a chest wound and one head wound." I watched as Sealyn stirred and then sat up, holding her head. "This one here looks pretty bad."

He was talking about me. Fucker. He's lucky I'm already gone. You're not supposed to say shit so the victim can hear. Di was screaming. Trish. Everybody. "Miss, you've got to move back!" The Police Officer had to pick Mianya up and carry her out of the room so the medical technician could at least try to do something for me. Mimi kept coming back though. There was complete pandemonium. The Polezei and the paramedics kept right on screaming. Screaming commands.

## Chapter 20

"Come on, baby! Wake up. Wake up, Dahni. Fight, Dahni! Wake up!"

"What is Mianya talking about?" I wondered as I rode my tricycle in the front yard. "Gramma! Look at me!" I was riding with no hands like my big brothers. Ma was on the porch snapping string beans.

"Look where you're going, Dahni. Be careful." Careful, Ma? I'm an X-treme biker:

*"Dahni."*

*"Yes, ma'am?"* My grandmother called me over and started talking to me. *"You know you have to go back, baby."*

## Don't Ask, Don't Tell

*"Ma'am, please. Why do I have to go back? I want to stay here with you."*
*"You can't stay here, baby. You have to go back. You have lots to do…"*
*"Yes Ma'am. Ma why does Mimi keep calling me?"*

*"Answer her, Dahni. See what she wants."*

"What's… the matter…, Mi-mi?" Shit, my throat hurt. I sounded like a dying frog.

"Dahni! Dahni!" Damn. The woman was screaming again.

"Why are you screaming? Where are you? I can't see you."

"Open your eyes, baby." I felt Mianya holding my hand. "Open, your eyes, Dahni." I tried.

"Is my grandmamma still here?" Silence.

"Uh, no baby. She's not here." I recognized Trish's silhouette.

"Trish," I said. "Trish, get Diana and Mimi. Don't let them come into the house."

Mimi lovingly squeezed my hand. "Baby, we're not at the house. We're at the hospital." Really?

"Who's sick?" I asked. Everybody laughed.

# Dahni McPhail

After a few moments I could hold open my eyes and actually see Trish, Diana, Mimi, Sanders, Bri, Adrian, Krys, Benson, Howard, Dorsey and Peaches. They were all crammed in the room with me and they were all looking like hell warmed over. What was wrong with them?

"What is wrong with all of you?" I croaked. "Why do y'all look like somebody steam rolled you?" They laughed again.

"Baby do you remember anything?" A slight pause and I remembered the last thing I saw before I talked to my grandmother.

"Mimi," I paused to get my thoughts together. "T is mad." I looked at Trish. "Trish, you have to get T. She's drinking again and she's mad." Trish turned around and walked out of the room. Diana went after her. "Yeah. Somebody go and get T..." My voice trailed off.

The next time I opened my eyes, I was in the room alone except for Mianya. She was lying asleep in the chair, right by my side. I turned my head toward her. "Mimi." She jumped straight up out of the chair. "I'm hungry."

She smiled. "Dahni! Dahni, baby! You're hungry!" Now, she was laughing and crying. "Yes! Yes! Thank you, Lord! My little piggy is hungry!"

The next couple of days brought physical, mental and emotional pain and some joy. On the third day, I got up and did a few things. I was so exhausted. Everything was hard to do but I was making great advances. That's when Mianya decided to tell me what happened to me.

"Baby, you were shot in the chest trying to push Sealyn out of harm's way." Then silence. I thought about that last episode.

"Yeah. Where's T, baby? Where is Sealyn? And Kelly? Are they OK?" When tears flowed from Mimi's eyes, I knew the answer to my question was not going to be good.

"Baby, Kelly didn't make it. Neither did T." Mianya reminded me that Kelly was dead before we entered the house. Then T tried to shoot Sealyn, but I pushed her out of the way and took the bullet. When T saw she shot me instead, she thought she killed me too and went ballistic. She stood at point blank range in front of Sealyn and fired but somehow only grazed Sealyn's head. The force of the shot knocked Sealyn out for a few minutes. Then T put the gun in her mouth and pulled the trigger. T was pronounced dead on the scene.

"Oh no. I have to get out of here!" I struggled trying to get out of the bed and leave. "I have to get my uniform ready to go to the funeral. T was my drill sergeant, Mimi! I have to be there!" Tears burned my eyes and rolled down my cheeks. It was the first time SFC Jones ever made me cry. I kept trying to get up. Mianya grabbed me and held me, sobbing gently.

"Dahni, the funeral is over. Baby, everything is over. You've been in a coma for a month."

## Chapter 21

A month? I'd been asleep for a month? How the hell could somebody sleep for that long? "Baby, your heart stopped while you were in the house. There were several times the doctors thought that you weren't going to make it." Shit, I *was* dead. I knew I was sitting on that chandelier.

"Where is everybody, Mimi?"

"They're all at home, changing. They supported us throughout this entire ordeal. They took off work just to sit by your bed in shifts. Even Adrian and Krys. Dahni, they're your real friends. I thought I was going to have to ask the doctor to sedate them, they were so upset in here."

"Nobody recorded them crying? I would have paid money to see that!" I chuckled.

"I see you're getting back to your silly self, baby! That's what I'm talking about."

"Trish and Diana?"

"Dahni, Trish took everything very hard. She saw it all happen and had to go to counseling, but she is maintaining. She barely moved from the side of this bed the entire time you've been here."

"That's whassup!"

"Mianya?"

"Yes, baby?"

I was almost afraid to ask. "Sealyn?"

Mianya's eyes filled with tears again. "Dahni, Sealyn—"

"Oh no! Sealyn's dead too??? I thought you said—"

"She's not dead, baby. We don't know where she is. She got up and walked out of the hospital. None of us has seen or heard from her since."

## Chapter 21

I stayed in the hospital two more weeks and then I was released. I gathered my things together in my room and waited on the bed for Mimi to come back and pick me up from the hospital.

"Ms. McPhail, this was just delivered for you."

It was a padded envelope with a stateside postmark. I opened it and reached in. I ran my fingers across an item that was sickeningly familiar. I knew what it was before I pulled it out of the bag. Mike's Rolex. I looked at the watch at length. Every diamond. Every crack and crevice. Then, I turned the watch over and read the inscription.

"I told you. I will do anything for you. ILY4EVA."

I dropped the watch on the floor.

## Don't Ask, Don't Tell

I was free from that hospital bed but that was about it. I still had a lot of therapy to go through. To help with my recovery, the military transferred me to Watkins Ring Medical Center in DC. Watkins Ring is the best military hospital available and provided cutting edge technology and treatment to ensure I got back to one hundred percent.

A short while after I got there, I bought my own condominium. Mianya was able to get orders and come with me which was highly improbable but extra great. This was our new duty station and everything in Germany was far behind.

I fully expected a long and drawn out investigation after everything that happened. When there is a hint of homosexuality involved in a tragic situation, some of the people assigned to the cases go the extra mile to discharge anyone they find engaging in those activities. To our surprise, we didn't have to go through that bullshit. They didn't conduct the "witch-hunt" to try to put us out or anything. What a relief.

Everything was good and Mimi and I were back in the states together. DC is nice. There is a lot of family in these parts. We met a few new friends and since our move Mianya ran into a couple of old friends that she used to be in a band with. I didn't know anything about that, but I will find out more, I'm sure.

There is always so much to see and do in DC. We have lots of fun visiting the historical monuments, shopping, going clubbing and of course, the food. Mimi and I were taking it all in and enjoying it together.

## Dahni McPhail

The other day when Mianya and I were getting some seafood at the wharf, I thought I saw Sealyn out of the corner of my eye. I tapped Mianya on the shoulder so she could look, but by the time we both turned our heads again, the woman was gone.

That night, I sat down in front of my computer to do some research. I found myself doing anything but that. I went to a search engine to look up a word that was on my mind:

> *PSYCHOPATH: person suffering from mental aberrations and disorders, especially one who perceives reality clearly except for his or her own social or moral obligations and seeks instant gratification in criminal or otherwise abnormal behavior.*

The word described Sealyn's heartless ass. I thought about how T left everything she owned to Sealyn along with an insurance policy worth over four hundred and fifty thousand dollars. I thought about the fact that Sealyn was a liar and a conniving individual without remorse. I wouldn't doubt that maniac was somewhere kicking it and enjoying her new life and newfound freedom while T lay in the cold ground.

"Dahni, come to bed. You know you're going to be screaming about getting up early for therapy tomorrow morning."

"OK, Mimi. Here I come, baby." I shut down my computer, laid in bed with my wife and went to sleep.

## Chapter 22

"Miss Jones, this is the luxury condominium for you! It has all the latest stainless steel appliances. There's 1500 square feet of space. Washer and dryer. You couldn't ask for a better condo in Dupont Circle or Washington D.C.!" The savvy realtor went on and on about the great deal her customer would get if she purchased the property.

"You're right, Beverly. I think I'll take this. Will you draw up the papers for me tonight? I'll come by and sign tomorrow. Let me write out my name for you. A lot of people spell it the way it sounds. But there's no "H" in my name. It's spelled S-E-A-L-Y-N—not Shawlyn—Jones. . ."

Dahni McPhail

# Your Friend Who Is

# Currently or

# Used To Be In The Military

# Will Love

# A Copy Of

# <u>Don't Ask, Don't Tell</u>

Can be ordered anywhere books are sold in all formats.

Contact Dahni at

dahnimcphail@yahoo.com

www.dahnimac.com